Praise for *Sixty Seconds*

"*Sixty Seconds* is fluent in its portrayal of European World War II culture and language with highly distinctive and flavorful characters, some virtuous, some evil, but all enjoyable. It is a panoramic epic loaded with wit, love, justice, and patriotism, taking place at the climax of the World War II era which has defined history ever after. It is a tale of great suffering when the world lost its head, aflame at the hands of destructive monsters who scorched the lives of undeserving millions, but, in spite of all, author Steven Mayfield has led us to a redemption at the end of that war's road. Finally, it is a story that reminds us of the greatness of America which has always been—and perhaps still is—a haven for the downtrodden and the forsaken, giving us hope by reminding us of the robust roots that anchor this nation's historical past and which promise to save us as an anchor for our inscrutable future."

—Jeff Schnader, award-winning author of *The Serpent Papers*

"Steven Mayfield's gripping novella follows nine curiously linked characters through the final moments of May 7, 1945, the end of World War II in Europe. Tension abounds as older readers connect these characters' experiences with those of their own relatives, while younger readers find themselves pulled into a world that, although eighty years in the past, still shapes our lives today."

—Karla Huebner, author of *In Search of the Magic Theater*

Also by Steven Mayfield

Howling at the Moon
Treasure of the Blue Whale
Delphic Oracle, USA
The Penny Mansions

SIXTY SECONDS

Steven Mayfield

Regal House Publishing

Copyright © 2025 Steven Mayfield. All rights reserved.

Published by
Regal House Publishing, LLC
Raleigh, NC 27605
All rights reserved

ISBN -13 (paperback): 9781646035977
ISBN -13 (epub): 9781646035984
Library of Congress Control Number: 2024944621

Cover images and design by © C. B. Royal
Author photo by Hunnicutt Photography

The following is a work of fiction created by the author. All names, individuals, characters, places, items, brands, events, etc. are either the product of the author's imagination or are used fictitiously. Any resemblance to actual events, places, institutions, persons, current or past, is entirely coincidental.

All rights reserved. No part of this publication may be reproduced, stored in a retrieval system, or transmitted, in any form or by any means, electronic, mechanical, photocopying, recording, or otherwise, without the prior permission of Regal House Publishing.

All efforts were made to determine the copyright holders and obtain their permissions in any circumstance where copyrighted material was used. The publisher apologizes if any errors were made during this process, or if any omissions occurred. If noted, please contact the publisher and all efforts will be made to incorporate permissions in future editions.

Regal House Publishing supports rights of free expression and the value of copyright. The purpose of copyright is to encourage the creation of artistic works that enrich and define culture.

Printed in the United States of America

Regal House Publishing, LLC
https://regalhousepublishing.com

This book is dedicated to artist Eva Claire (Roeder) MacLowry who was spirited out of Nazi Germany in 1938 as a three-year-old just months before Kristallnacht (the Night of Broken Glass). Arriving in America on the Fourth of July, she was then raised in Buffalo, New York, studied at Pratt Institute in NYC, and married her high school sweetheart, Jim. Together, they built a life that went from Buffalo to New York City to Los Angeles to the NIH in Bethesda, MD before settling just down the street from my wife and me in Portland, Oregon. A marvelous painter, four of Eva's pieces now hang in my home, one evocative of the Holocaust and an inspiration for this book.

1

7 May 1945

1759:00 to 1759:10 Eastern Standard Time
2359:00 to 2359:10 Central European Time

Farley

From his glass-walled broadcast booth perched on the side of a temporary stage in Times Square, Farley Sackstead watched and listened to the girl with reddish hair as she stood before a phalanx of microphones. She was talented and at an age when the woman she would become was still hidden by a schoolgirl's pleated plaid skirt, bobby sox and loafers, and a spray of faint freckles around her nose. Already fifteen seconds into her performance, Farley was inclined to let her rendition of "The Star-Spangled Banner" stand on its own. The girl was an excellent singer, and better yet, had chosen to move through the song quickly, without unnecessary runs or notes held too long.

The broadcast enclosure was tiny with enough space for only two compartments, and as the young woman continued to sing, the sound engineer motioned at Farley through the glass separating their cubicles, one hand tapping the earpiece of his headset, the other flapping like the bill of a quacking duck. His lips moved, the words muted but unmistakable.

Say something!

The veteran broadcaster shook his head and the engineer then scribbled a message on the back of his script notes. He held it up against the glass for Farley to read.

Nobbie wants commentary!

Farley clenched his teeth. Former sports announcer and

current director of ad sales Nobbie Wainwright was the producer for the broadcast because everyone else in management wanted the night off to celebrate the eve of V-E Day. Nobbie liked telling other people what to do and had a lot of ideas on how a straight news radio program was supposed to play out. He'd not been shy about sharing his views with Farley, acting as if the wartime voice of CBS Radio in Europe was a cub reporter. Nobbie's biggest beef was with "The Star-Spangled Banner." In his baseball play-by-play days he'd favored the traditional mid-seventh inning "God Bless America," a hymn he'd routinely sung to a wincing radio audience at the top of his lungs and off-key. He wanted Farley to add commentary that would elbow the national anthem into the background if not off the air altogether. "Talk about the crowd size or something, Sackstead," he'd told him during the production meeting that morning. "Or ad lib one of those preachy things you used to close out your London broadcasts. Add some gravitas."

"It's the national anthem, Nobbie," Farley had countered. "I think it's got enough gravitas of its own."

"'…whose broad stripes and bright stars,'" the girl sang as the sound engineer continued to quack with one hand, encouraging Farley to underscore the performance. Farley sighed, then nodded. He didn't like Nobbie Wainwright but agreed with him on one thing. The national anthem should be "God Bless America," an evocative melody with lyrics more representative of the country. Farley considered "The Star-Spangled Banner" to be the tuneful version of a stutter, pauses and run-on phrasing necessary to match words and music.

He reached out and switched on his microphone, then spoke in his low distinctive voice, employing the familiar idiosyncratic cadence his listeners found both trustworthy and reassuring.

"As we listen to fifteen-year-old Jenny Doyle from Queens, New York, sing 'The Star-Spangled Banner,' it is a moment of both joy and sadness…of profound gratitude and profound regret."

"'…through the perilous fight.'"

"Let us never forget those who gave their lives that we may all be free and pray God the world will never again be embroiled in a conflict of this magnitude."

The sound engineer replaced his quacking duck with a circular motion, one finger extended as if he twirled a tiny hoop on it, his lips again moving.

Keep it going!

Farley frowned. The impossibly young technician had too much hair and too little respect for his elders, treating Farley as if this were his first broadcast. It was annoying and Farley wanted to mute his microphone long enough to remind him that the anchorman of *This is London* had likely forgotten more about broadcast journalism than this snot-nosed little fart from NYU would ever know. The veteran newsman was on the air and didn't do it—wouldn't have, anyway, because of Marta. "Be patient, liebchen," Farley's Austrian-born wife had gently reminded him when he called during the most recent commercial break. "I seem to remember another snot-nosed little fart who knew more about everything than everyone."

The engineer plastered more instructions from Nobbie against the smudged glass that separated him from Farley, his twirling finger picking up speed.

"'O'er the ramparts...'"

"And now..." Farley intoned, ignoring the engineer in favor of the upturned faces that filled the streets and plaza below the stage. "I'll be quiet and listen along with those of you beside your radios here in New York, in America, and across the world as the final countdown begins to V-E Day. I'm Farley Sackstead. This is CBS radio."

Selma

"Here kitty, kitty, kitty," Selma Filbert called out. A chorus of meows sounded, one cat atop a kitchen cabinet, another crawling out from a rip in the underside lining of the box springs in her bedroom, a third from inside one of Carl's boots, the rest from every corner of her small house. "We've got some new guests," she told her favorite from among the Sidneys. The calico glanced at the nearest newcomer and hissed. "Don't be like that, dear," Selma scolded him. A bag of dry cat food was on the kitchen table, a metal measuring cup inside. She went to it, retrieved a couple of scoops, and then scattered them across the kitchen floor. It provoked a feeding frenzy, the cats whining and yowling as they scrambled after the food. Selma smiled with satisfaction. No matter how many cats were in her family the night before, mornings seemed to add another, a flap Carl had installed in the back door for their long-departed dog serving as an invitation to homeless feline immigrants. *Carl would hate it,* Selma thought. He'd hated cats.

"But I love you," Selma said as the cats battled each other over the kibble. "And who would take care of you if I weren't here?"

Earlier that day a policeman had been at the door. Again. "There's been some concern about your cats, ma'am," he'd claimed. "I'd like to get a look inside if that's okay."

"It *isn't* okay!"

"Ma'am, please let me come in. Otherwise, I'll just get a search warrant."

"You've got no probable cause for a search warrant."

Selma knew about probable cause. After the first policeman dispatched by the Voice, she'd retrieved her long winter overcoat from its hanger on the front porch, donned it even though the day was approaching eighty degrees, and walked to Rockefeller Center, afterward taking a bus down Fifth Avenue to reach the free legal clinic at the law school. A nice young law student with more acne than whiskers had listened to her complaint and then told her about probable cause.

"I know my rights and you gotta have probable cause," she'd shouted at the cop. "Which you *haven't* got! Now go away!"

And he had.

The radio in the parlor was on, a woman singing "The Star-Spangled Banner." She sounded young, her voice clear. She'd been singing for fifteen or twenty seconds.

"'...through the perilous fight.'"
I had a good voice too. Mrs. Birdicko picked me to sing the solo.

Selma had frozen that day, terrified by the expectant faces in the audience waiting for her to perform. Eventually Mrs. Birdicko, her sixth-grade music teacher with the kind eyes, had emerged from the wing and gently led her off the stage.

The food Selma had scattered about was gone, the scramble abating as some of her cats made for one of several pans filled with malodorous sand, others slipping through the dog door, a few seeking privacy in corners and then defecating on the kitchen floor.

"No, no, dears," Selma softly scolded the squatting cats. She retrieved a paper towel, sank to her knees on the cracked linoleum, and began to clean up the feces, nose wrinkled, a pinched expression forming when the song coming from her radio in the next room was joined by the Voice.

"It is a moment of both joy and sadness, of profound gratitude and profound regret..."

Selma rose, wincing when her arthritic hips protested, then made for the parlor where the radio sat unevenly on a displaced kitchen chair. She crossed to it, at the same time retrieving a tiny container of Miracle Holy Water from the pocket of her housecoat. She'd received her latest allotment of the precious stuff from Reverend Woodrow Dodge only that morning, a two-ounce vial with a picture of Jesus on the label. It came in a padded envelope with a prayer card and a request from the radio pastor for more money. She twisted off the vial's cap and sprinkled water on the radio. The Voice was undeterred. Caramel smooth and rich, his timbre evoked temptation incarnate.

"...listening along with those of you beside your radios here in New York..."

"I know where his laboratory is. That's where you'll find him," she'd promised Riley before sending him off on his mission. She'd given the boy Carl's pistol and the special bullets. She hoped it would be enough. If not, more Miracle Holy Water would be needed and Selma made for the kitchen drawer where she kept her checkbook, scattering cats in every direction as she plowed through them. The words of the Voice followed her, stinking of sulfur and sin as they poured from the radio.

"…in America, and across the world as the final countdown begins to V-E Day. I'm Farley Sackstead."

Jenny

Jenny Doyle was more than twenty seconds into the song. The high notes were still ahead, but so far her voice hadn't wavered. About sixty seconds were left if she followed her father's advice. "The damned thing shouldn't last more than one and a half minutes. The season'll be over by the time she's done," Brian Doyle griped when one of the prima donnas the Yankees had hired to perform the anthem before games took twice as long to warble through the convoluted lyrics. This was not Jenny's first performance of "The Star-Spangled Banner" before a large crowd. She'd stood on the pitcher's mound and sung before a Yankees game the previous September, chosen after an audition in front of new owners MacPhail, Topping, and Webb. She'd been the youngest to try out and the only one without formal training—the other aspirants experienced vocalists, some from Broadway and one from the chorus of the Metropolitan Opera company. But Jenny took the day, her voice pure and truthful, her range enviable. The Yankees' owners unanimously picked her, and when the night arrived she hadn't missed a note. The bored crowd politely cheered after she was finished, their cries crescendoing to an ovation when their beloved Yankees streamed onto the field for the top half of the first. The players had trotted past Jenny as she made her way off the diamond. Shortstop Frankie Crosetti, her favorite player, winked at her. "One minute, twenty-two seconds," Dad proudly revealed after she joined him in the stands. The Bronx Bombers won that day, beating the White Sox nine to eight. Dad credited her performance.

Tonight was different. Tonight Jenny Doyle wasn't at Yankee Stadium, standing before a few thousand baseball fans with hands over their hearts, the urge to gleefully hurl insults at the umpires dampened by obligatory respect for their nation's anthem. Tonight she was on the radio and the world was listening.

As six o'clock approached and afternoon in New York City eased into evening, there were more tears than cheers coming from the crowd gathered in a plaza created by the junction of Broadway, Seventh Avenue, and Forty-Second Street. They cried with relief and joy, with longing and grief. Jenny did not cry. She could not. Her voice might fail if she cried and she'd vowed to keep it strong. For the radio microphones. For America and the world. For Jimmy.

A row of chairs filled with dignitaries was behind her, Mayor LaGuardia among the notables. Dad didn't like him, had voted for O'Dwyer in '41. "Brian Doyle ain't never voted for a wop and he ain't never gonna," he'd vowed. Still, LaGuardia was the mayor and Jenny Doyle was a pipe fitter's daughter from Queens, so she'd demurely taken Hizzoner's hand when they were introduced. "I'm very pleased to meet you, sir," she'd told him. LaGuardia had been immensely impressed to get respect from an Irish girl and winked. Then the announcer called her name. "Please stand and remove your hats for our national anthem, performed tonight by fifteen-year-old Jenny Doyle from Queens, New York."

She'd practiced over and over, determined that her rendition would not exceed one minute and thirty seconds—that she would reach her final held note at six p.m., coinciding with midnight in Europe and the official end of war with Hitler's Germany. But the mayor's wink before she began, her name echoing across Times Square from the public address system, and the imposing cluster of microphones at center stage had been momentarily unnerving. She'd frozen, losing three seconds before the reverent, upturned faces in the crowd restored her confidence and she was able to begin—her voice steady and assured even though this wasn't Yankee Stadium on a balmy Wednesday night in September; even though it was Times

Square, the war was about to officially end, and Jenny Doyle from Queens had been picked to sing the national anthem live to thousands amassed in the plaza and via radio to millions across the world.

Jenny surveyed the crowd as she sang, making eye contact with the most receptive faces, just as Mrs. Petroff at John Adams High had taught her. Soldiers from all the services peppered the throng and she was again reminded of Jimmy. His uniform had been crisp, his face unlined when his train pulled away in '43, the grin on his face so different from the unexpected photo Bridget had discovered in *Life* magazine. Jenny's best friend had run all the way from her home on Killarney to the Doyle residence off Huron and 155th that day, holding up the magazine when Jenny answered the banging on the front door.

"Look at this!"

And there it was on the cover: Jenny's brother, Jimmy Doyle, and his fellow crewmen stood in front of their B-17 bomber—the *Daisy Mae*—cartoonist Al Capp's heroine with the hourglass figure painted on the nose alongside twenty-five tiny bombs, each representing a successful mission. Seventeen years old with an easy grin when he left for Europe, Jimmy in the photo had just turned eighteen, but his face in the picture was older. He wasn't grinning. None of the men were. That was more than a year and twenty-one tiny bombs ago.

Jimmy...

Jenny felt her voice tremble, stumbled on the next lyric, then regained her composure and pressed on. "'O'er the ramparts...'" she sang as the second hand on a huge clock mounted at the rear of the stage crossed over the *2*. She was on schedule. Her performance and the war in Europe would both be over in fifty seconds.

Stangl

Stangl lay on his bunk, staring at the ceiling. *I did my part!* he fumed. And yet none of it had gone as planned. The car hadn't come even though the former commandant of the death camp at Sobibor had arrived at the appointed place exactly on time, his beloved and distinctive uniform exchanged for the ill-fitting gray suit provided by Hudal's man.

Without a tie! Did they not know who I am?

They'd known at Sobibor and Treblinka. He'd done good work there, efficient work. The nasty business at Sobibor was after he left, and yet many in SS command blamed him, claiming he'd left lax security in place for the new commandant.

Lax security! One hundred thousand or more cleansed during my tenure. No one complained about lax security then!

After the Americans captured him in Vienna, Stangl had been unceremoniously transported to Linz, Austria, in the back of a troop carrier, the only passenger in the cavernous rear bed of a vehicle designed to carry twenty-five soldiers. They'd left before dawn, the chilly early morning air flapping the truck's canvas siding. Shivering and miserable by the time they reached their destination, Stangl had been happy to exchange the truck for the stockade even though his current six-by-eight-foot room with its cinderblock walls and narrow bunk was hardly the accommodation an SS officer of his stature deserved. Three days had elapsed since then.

The radio was on in the guardroom outside the cellblock, the sound carrying through an open door. The guards played it day and night, turning up the volume if he complained. Fortunately they mostly listened to music rather than news reports: romantic ballads from Frank Sinatra, wistful lilts from Dinah Shore, jazzy instrumentals by the Benny Goodman Quartet or Glenn Miller's orchestra. A few minutes earlier a tune by Miller's band—"In the Mood"—had played. Miller had been a favorite of Stangl's before the war, and even though the SS officer publicly shared the Führer's disapproval of American music, he'd privately mourned when the trombonist's plane went missing. After "In the Mood" ended, the guards had picked up the CBS Radio feed, and now a female singer was a few measures into the national anthem of the United States.

Suddenly the voice of the famous American broadcaster,

Farley Sackstead, intruded upon her performance. "It will be a moment of both joy and sadness, of profound gratitude and profound regret…"

Stangl didn't understand much English, but Sackstead's tone was unmistakable. It was the voice of a gracious victor. The former SS officer scowled in the darkness of his tiny cell. *"Taunt the conquered,"* the Führer had encouraged his disciples. *"Be proud in victory."* And Stangl had gladly obeyed the directive, taking great pride in his work on behalf of the Reich, particularly at Sobibor. He'd arrived at the camp in 1942 to find the processing disorganized and quickly established order: two lines upon arrival, the shorter one destined for the workers' barracks, the other for the chambers in Lager III. The monthly numbers had subsequently ballooned, a result he'd found immensely satisfying. *The precision and order of it all,* he'd written his wife, Theresa. *The indisputable logic. The finality. It's like taking out the trash. What is purged is forever gone and no longer stinks.* As time went on, however, he'd lost interest and by the end of his brief tour rarely left his bivouac and the company of his maid, Gosia, unless it was to venture out to nearby Wlodawa in the back seat of his staff car. There was one good restaurant there and he'd especially enjoyed their pierogi and polskie naleśniki, even though the rich cuisine played havoc with his bowels.

Stangl frowned, his face dimly illuminated by light from a single overhead bulb in the outer corridor of the cellblock. It shone through the open view slit of an otherwise solid door, bringing with it the earnest, dignified voice of Farley Sackstead from the radio in the guardroom. Stangl gritted his teeth. The once glorious mission of the Third Reich would end ignominiously in less than a minute, the aftermath of the conflict that had consumed Europe and the world for five-and-a-half long, bloody years a radical departure from its inception—no Panzer tanks triumphantly rampaging across borders, no Wehrmacht paratroopers dropping from the sky like winged Goth warriors. Instead, disarmed men in raggedy uniforms were already making their way back to homes they hoped had survived, disconsolately plodding along bomb-ravaged roads and past confused refugees, their square-jawed pride replaced by despair. Indeed, all the proud victories of the German people were about to be rewarded with nothing more than retribution. *I'll probably hang*, Stangl mused, the once-feared man known as the "White Death" dangling from the gibbet like a dried chicken.

Unless Hudal can intervene…get me out of here.

The woman on the radio sang on, her voice gaining confidence. She sounded young—perhaps not a woman, like Gosia, but a girl. He rolled onto his side in the bunk, conjuring an image of his maid at Sobibor, imagining that she lay next to him, her body warm.

"…as the final countdown begins to V-E Day."

The low, somber voice of the American broadcaster on the radio dragged him from Gosia's embrace, abruptly returning him to his cold cell with its concrete floor and damp cinderblock walls. The mattress on his bunk was thin, the pillow starved of feathers even thinner. Nevertheless, Stangl held it against his chest, spooning with it as if the pillow were Gosia, imagining he could feel and hear her breathing as the girl on the radio sang, her performance underscored by Farley Sackstead's unwelcome commentary.

Jimmy

Jimmy Doyle strolled up the dark road, heading back to Feucht Airfield outside Nuremberg, Germany, an unlit cigarette dangling from his lips. It was part of his plan to quit smoking. "Du rauchst zu viel," a whore had told him. "Sie stinken danach." Jimmy had an excellent memory and grasp of accents, repeating the words perfectly when he later saw Antoni, the interpreter. "'You smoke too much. You reek of it,'" Antoni had translated for him, his English offering merely a hint of his native Poland. Afterward Jimmy tried to quit, cold turkey, but it was impossible. Every night, after two or three beers in a Nuremberg rathskeller, he bummed a smoke that led to another and another and then a pack he later picked up from the commissary. *Jenny would hate it*, he mused. She believed cigarettes ruined a good singing voice. His sister was four years younger and four thousand miles away, yet he could feel her presence.

I'm trying, Jenny.

Cap had quit smoking by constantly chewing gum while occasionally taking a drag from an unlit cigarette, inhaling deeply as if the divine essence of tobacco could be captured without the evil of its demonic smoke. "I ain't lit me a butt in two months," the tall West Virginian claimed, urging Jimmy to give it a try. Jimmy had taken the advice and so far it was working. He took a pull from his unlit cigarette, then tossed it into the high grass bordering the roadway. It was a beautiful night—quiet, cool, and nearly windless. He tested out his singing voice, launching lyrics from Cole Porter's "Night and Day" into the air.

The hoot of an owl silenced the young airman, reminding him that the official end of hostilities wouldn't begin for another minute or so, even though a ceasefire was supposedly in place. "Renegade Krauts are out there," Cap had repeatedly warned Jimmy and the rest of his crew, recommending they stay inside the fences at the temporary American airbase a few kilometers east of Nuremberg. "Most o' them German boys wanna surrender to 'Mericans 'stead o' Russians," Cap had conceded. "But I hear tell a few think ol' Adolph give 'em a license to keep huntin'." It was sound logic Jimmy had disregarded every night for more than a week now. The *Daisy Mae*'s belly gunner spent much of his day curled into the cramped underside turret of their B-17. "I need to stretch my legs a bit, Cap," he told the command pilot of their bomber before heading out each night. "I'll be careful."

Despite the end of bombing runs the *Daisy Mae* was still flying. Jimmy and his crewmates continued to rise in the fog of early morning, and after chow, don fleece-lined coats and boots before climbing into their Flying Fortress where Jimmy stuffed himself into the belly turret. "You'll love the view without all the ack-ack," their ground-crew chief had promised, but the young belly gunner hadn't liked it at all in the beginning. His reliable twin 0.50-caliber machine guns had been removed and replaced with a camera, and with nothing but Plexiglas separating him from the vast sky and the ground below, it had felt as if he were about to plunge earthward at any moment. At least with the twin 0.50s, he'd had something substantial to grab if the turret catastrophically came loose from the plane...or inexplicably evaporated.

Jimmy was on the return leg of his nightly walk, Feucht Airfield still an eighth of a mile away. The road was dark, save beams of light from the base spotlights that illuminated a sharp leftward bend fifty yards ahead. He looked at the watch purchased in Nuremberg from a German wearing a once-expensive but now tattered suit. It had cost him a dollar and a pack of cigarettes. "Es ist ein Stowa," the old man told him, weeping when he handed over the timepiece. The brand name had meant nothing to Jimmy. He'd wanted the watch because of its luminous hands, both now pointed up.

Jenny!

"Dammit!" he muttered. Her letter had arrived a few days earlier and he'd planned to be back before she began, but the night had been peaceful and his mind had wandered.

Dear Jimmy,

You'll never guess what's happened. I've been picked to sing The Star-Spangled Banner in Times Square on May 7th. They're going to broadcast it on the radio all over the world. You'll be able to hear me wherever you are as long as there's a radio around. It'll start just before six o'clock in the evening here in New York. I don't know what time that will be where you are.

Jimmy stopped. Without the sound of his boots against the pavement he could hear Jenny's voice coming from distant loudspeakers. "You should hear my sister sing," he'd bragged to his buddies on the *Daisy Mae* after sharing the letter with them. "Mark my words...one day Jenny's gonna be on the radio." And now it was true, her broadcasted performance enriching a night otherwise eerily quiet, her mezzo-soprano voice exactly as he remembered.

No… It's better.

He stopped to listen, his eyes welling with tears—not for the anthem and the nation—but for the little sister he'd not seen in so long. Her delivery of melody and lyrics were assured—no longer tentative in the shy, breathy way of a girl but with the confidence of a woman; indeed, while Jimmy Doyle had been away transforming from a boy to a man, his little sister had apparently grown up too.

"Pray God we never again see the world embroiled in a conflict of this magnitude," the radio commentator added to Jenny's performance. His voice was familiar, his words professionally articulated. "…And as we listen to fifteen-year-old Jenny Doyle from Queens, New York, sing 'The Star-Spangled Banner'…."

The man continued to offer commentary in hushed tones, Jimmy struggling to tune him out, listening only for his sister's voice—sweet, pure, innocent, brave.

"And now, I'll be quiet, listening along with those of you beside your radios here in London, in America, and across the world," the man at last intoned.

"Then *be* the fuck quiet," Jimmy muttered.

Gosia

Malgorzata "Gosia" Pietkowski grasped the bedsheets knotted to the footboard, closed her eyes, lifted her shoulders, and pushed as hard as she could. The baby refused to move.

Stubborn…like Antoni.

"Push!" the midwife exhorted. "Just push, Gosia, push!"

The contraction began to fade, but Gosia kept pushing, trying not to scream lest the frustrated midwife again scold her in English that Gosia's aunt would have to translate into Polish.

"Don't scream, You're giving up the power in your push if you scream."

The midwife was in her forties, desperately trying to reclaim her twenties, and had arrived at the apartment above the delicatessen in a party dress, anxious to join the crowds celebrating V-E Day in Times Square. Her name was Rita. She didn't like her job. She didn't like foreigners. She didn't like Gosia. She didn't hide her opinions.

"Just push, dammit! Stop screaming!"

The contraction was nearly gone, but Gosia squeezed her eyes more tightly shut, held her breath, and continued to push. A whimper escaped her lips, leaking out like air from a punctured tire. She looked at Rita, pleading with her eyes to make it all stop—to pull out the baby through her belly button if necessary. Instead, the midwife frowned as her hand on Gosia's abdomen felt the contraction dissipating.

"Lift your butt," she said.

Gosia looked at her aunt.

"Podnieś tyłek, kochanie," Ewa told her niece. *Lift your bottom, dear.*

Gosia lifted her hips off the mattress, closing her eyes as Rita used a wet cloth to clean her, afterward replacing the paper pad used to protect the bedding. She wrapped the soiled cloth in the old pad and then handed it to Ewa, wrinkling her nose.

"Przykro mi," Gosia said. *I'm sorry.*

"I don't understand Polack."

"I...sorry."

"Whatever... You all do it." The midwife pinched her nose shut with two fingers. "Jesus, it stinks in here."

It was true. The room stank of Gosia's sweat and her shit, and she was embarrassed even though Aunt Ewa had warned it could happen. Gosia's aunt had given birth to four children, all now grown, and after her niece's arrival two months earlier had gently explained what to expect during childbirth. "You might have a bowel movement, Gosia, but don't worry about it," she'd reassured her niece. "It's nothing to be ashamed of. Your baby is making room to get out. I did it too."

The contraction was fully spent, the room now quiet save the voice of a girl on the radio singing the American national anthem.

"'...bright stars through...'"

Earlier, Uncle Jakub had relocated the countertop radio from the kitchen to the studio where Gosia now labored, afterward pulling his wife aside for an exchange of whispers. Fragments of their conversation had been loud enough for Gosia to hear.

"How will…"

"I don't…"

"HIAS?"

Gosia knew about HIAS—the Hebrew Immigrant Aid Society—knew, as well, that her aunt and uncle couldn't afford a doctor and hospital if she were unable to push her baby out. "No doctor, no hospital," she'd told them. "I'll keep trying." And she had, pushing with each contraction for the last hour. It was no use. The baby refused to descend.

Stubborn, stubborn baby…

Gosia wished Antoni were there. Her husband would have found a way to distract her, to make the insistent pain less ferocious. An honest man, he was a good liar when a good lie was needed. At Sobibor he'd lied to her every day until the revolt, reassuring his wife each morning that the Americans would soon liberate them. *"Don't give up, Gosia. They will be here today,"* he'd promised, pivoting when evening came and SS guards still manned their machine guns in the watchtowers. *"Don't worry. The Americans will be here tomorrow."*

"'…the perilous fight…'" the girl on the radio continued. She had a lovely soprano voice, although her song was uncomfortably reminiscent of the marching-band music played when German soldiers goose-stepped into Warsaw, their steely Aryan chins pointed upward in triumph. Gosia and Antoni had been forced to bear witness that day, weeping openly as the jackbooted Nazis swaggered in step down the Nowy Swiat, provoking fear and grief, humiliation and regret. When news of German incursion into the Polish frontier reached them, Antoni had wanted both their families to make for the countryside where ragtag fragments of Poland's regular army were coalescing to organize a resistance. But Gosia's father had forbidden his daughter to leave, and despite her nascent marriage to Antoni, Father's decisions still ruled. "The family must stay togeth-

er," he'd insisted. "All this will pass. We must keep our heads down...not cause trouble." Gosia now both missed and hated her father, grieving his immediate assignment to Lager III after stumbling out of the railcar at Sobibor, angry with herself for listening to him rather than her husband.

"'O'er the ramparts...'" the girl on the radio went on as Gosia lay back on her pillow, the voice of the famous broadcaster, Farley Sackstead, underlining the singer's. He spoke in English Gosia could not understand although she recognized the gravity and portent in his tone. The war in Europe, although not officially over, was now history. The death camp at Sobibor, like her last contraction, was a memory too, and she once more wished that Antoni were at her bedside, knowing what he would tell her.

"Don't worry, Gosia. The baby will be here today."

Zimmer

The distant sound of a woman singing made Zimmer stumble and he once again cursed the dense obstacle course of gnarly, exposed roots, fallen trees, and thorny brambles. Even though the city of Nuremberg was nearby, its adjoining forest—the Lorenzer—was thick enough to be daunting in the timid light of a slivered moon. He stopped to listen. The words of the song were in English, the singer's accent American.

"'Whose broad stripes and bright stars...'"

There had been talk up and down the line for days before he and Braun deserted, all of it eventually funneling into a single rumor that streaked through the exhausted regiments: General Froetsch planned to surrender all troops between the Bohemian Forest and the Upper Inn River. "Surrender to whom?" Braun had sniffed. "Russians? They'll likely shoot us on the spot. Fuck Froetsch! We must get out of here... Make our own surrender." The two young Wehrmacht soldiers—combat veterans dating to the invasion of Poland—knew the US Army controlled Feucht Airfield near Nuremberg. "We'll go there and surrender to airmen," Braun decided for them both. "They haven't looked up our nostrils for the last five years. They're less likely to shoot us."

Zimmer had believed him. It was a habit, believing Braun. Fighting together on two fronts, separated by a few weeks after the uprising at Sobibor when their platoon was briefly diverted to help round up escapees, his friend had rarely been wrong. So they'd made for Feucht Airfield, staying together until earlier that day. Zimmer was alone now and wondered if Braun were still alive. Fifteen kilometers east of their destination they'd encountered a Russian patrol. Zimmer had been exhausted and hungry. He'd wanted to surrender and ignored Braun's advice. Pulling away from his friend's grasp, he'd stepped into the open from their hiding spot above the Russian soldiers, his hands raised.

"Wir geben auf. Nicht schießen." *We give up. Don't shoot.*

The Russians immediately opened fire and Zimmer and Braun had run for their lives, dodging massive boulders and leaping over fallen limbs as shots buzzed past their ears, kicked up dirt at their heels, and clipped small branches from the trees that pelted the two Wehrmacht soldiers like dead birds. Eventually one round produced the unmistakable thud of a bullet hitting solid flesh and he'd heard Braun go down. Zimmer hadn't turned back to help, hadn't even slowed because he knew Braun would not have stopped for him either. It was counter to the training they'd received after mustering into the Wehrmacht five and a half years earlier. "If the man next to you falls," their platoon sergeant had advised, "keep going unless you want to join him!"

Zimmer and Braun had been the last survivors from their original platoon of raw recruits. Now only Zimmer was left and the cumulative enormity of the loss made him stop at the edge of the forest, the roadway to Feucht Airfield thirty feet away and the height of an average man below. Looking up, he contemplated the night sky, seemingly enormous after hours in the dense forestation of the Lorenzer. Earlier that day, an American bomber had passed low overhead. "Getting ready to land," Braun had observed. "The American airfield must be close. We're going to make it." Now the sky was empty of both aircraft and clouds, allowing stars and their formations to possess the night.

Zimmer knew all the constellations. They'd taught the boys how to navigate by the stars in the Hitlerjugend. He'd been among the best of them and now searched for Ursa Major, recalling his instructor, Herr Grohe. "Find the seven brightest stars of Ursa Major, the papa bear," he'd taught his boys. "Those make up the Big Dipper. The two stars on the outside of the cup are the pointer stars. They'll direct you to the end of the tail on the Little Dipper. That's Polaris, the North Star." Most of the boys, save Engel, had very much liked Herr Grohe. Engel was a rabid little National Socialist constantly vigilant for traitors to the cause. Herr Grohe—gangly and bespectacled—was a reluctant Nazi, less embarrassed by the knobby knees that perturbed the hem of his khaki shorts than his armband with its prominent swastika. The camp counselor regretted joining the party, a confidence he'd inadvisably shared with the boys in his Section over a late-night campfire on one of their survival maneuvers. He'd made them promise to keep his secret, but the zealous Engel had promptly betrayed him and Herr Grohe disappeared, his quarters expeditiously occupied by a new man with less knowledge of astronomy and greater pride in his armband.

That's one thing about the party, Zimmer mused. *They were efficient.*

Zimmer found the North Star, then looked for Cassiopeia. The W-shaped constellation would be due west at midnight.

From there, Feucht Airfield is southwest.

He looked at his watch, amazed that its second hand continued to reliably complete its 360 degrees of arc. The timepiece with its scuffed leather wristband had been through hell since he'd scavenged it from a dead Russian officer. Shaken by mortar fire on the retreat from Leningrad, repeatedly slammed against the brick walls and cobblestone streets of Bautzen as they fought to hold the city against advancing Soviets, and then plunged underwater when he and Braun crossed the Pegnitz

River, its hands still shone in the dark. They were pointed nearly straight up. Less than one minute remained until midnight.

Riley

Riley Blaine fought his way through the crowd, several rows of the standing-room-only audience still separating him from the stage. He could see Jenny and hear her voice coming from the huge loudspeakers on the dais. On one side of the stage a glass booth had been constructed. Two men were inside, one half-standing. He wore headphones and held a piece of paper against the glass that bifurcated the transparent enclosure.

"Watch it, buddy!"

Riley looked to the voice. An unapologetically drunk sailor in dress blues glared at him. "Don't be crowdin' me," the swabbie added, afterward struggling unsuccessfully to sustain a frown that morphed into a wide grin. He slapped Riley on the back. "That's okay, pal. The war in Europe is over. Everything's okay now." He swayed drunkenly, shifting his attention to the girl standing next to him, a sandy haired beauty wearing a red dress with white polka dots.

"The war's over, sister. Howsabout a kiss?"

The young woman responded with a homicidal stare the inebriated sailor conveniently mistook as invitation. He grabbed her and planted a kiss on her lips, holding on until she got a handful of his ear and pulled. Yowling, he released her and she promptly belted him with a closed fist. The sailor fell back, his stunned expression quickly replaced by another grin.

"Helluva right hook, doll!" he exclaimed, rubbing his chin.

The girl answered by winding up again, but before she could launch another punch the sailor stumbled off, leaving her with a raised fist and no one to hit. She eyed Riley, glowering.

"Whaddayou lookin' at, buster?"

Riley bowed his head.

"I shoulda got here early," he murmured. "...before the crowd."

"What?"

Riley lifted his eyes enough to see her, then quickly lowered them back to the street. The girl was very pretty.

"She sent me to the wrong place," he mumbled. "The Cat Woman. She told me to wait outside the building and then sneak in."

The girl lowered her fist, cocking her head. "What's wrong with you anyway?" she asked. "You retarded or something?"

Riley's head jerked up. "I ain't—"

The girl cut him off by turning away, afterward edging through a crease in the crowd and then disappearing into a jumble of bodies. Riley looked up at Jenny. She stood at the center of the stage five feet above the street, her eyes surveying the huge gathering as she sang. It was almost time and he was still too far away.

It's not my fault! She sent me to the wrong place! I ain't retarded! I ain't no imbecile!

Earlier he'd wasted nearly an hour, hidden behind a dumpster in the parking lot outside CBS headquarters, waiting for a chance to slip into the building. "When people exit to the lot, the door doesn't lock unless it's shut hard," the Cat Woman had promised. "No one ever closes it right. You can get in."

"'…through the perilous fight,'" Jenny sang, the outdoor speakers lending an artificial warble to her voice that belied its natural clarity. On Riley's single night in the Doyle home she'd played the piano and sung "Someone to Watch Over Me," a pretty and sweet girl so unlike the two young women who'd exited the CBS building just an hour previous, one of them a natural redhead, the other literally dyeing to be. Riley had seen them before, watching from his perch atop the building across the parking lot. They were always laughing, their voices not musical, like Jenny's, but coarse and loud like the girls at School 87 in Buffalo—the popular and not so popular ones who'd taunted the boy born with a split lip, the repair drawing his mouth up at the center in a way that made him resemble a cat. Laughing and issuing high-pitched meows when he started across the gym floor at the eighth-grade dances, they were sirens with stuffed bras—girls who wanted the football players to whirl them around, to pull them close, to graze their soft bottoms with sweaty fingers.

Just as the Cat Woman predicted, the two women at the CBS building hadn't pushed the door shut, leaving it slightly ajar and then strolling to the middle of the parking lot where they'd talked for a few minutes. Everything was *so* funny.

"And then he said… Ha, ha, ha!"

"And then I told him… Ha, ha, ha!"

The redhead had lingered after her friend headed for the Fifty-Third Street subway station, and before long, Nobbie Wainwright drove up and parked his car next to the only other vehicle in the otherwise empty lot. He and the woman had greeted each other with indiscreet pawing. Afterward they'd gone into the CBS building together. Nobbie had been wearing his blue corduroy jacket with leather patches on its sleeves, reminding Riley of Pastor Wondercheck back in Buffalo. The pastor owned a brown one he typically paired with a turtleneck sweater. Both men—Nobbie Wainwright and Pastor Wondercheck—were tall and thick and mean. They both called Riley "Felix the cat." Pap had taunted Riley with the same nickname, lamenting that he'd been cursed with a slut for a wife and an idiot for a son. An engineman on one of the massive freighters that ferried grain, iron ore, and other commodities along the Great Lakes to and from the port at Buffalo, his disposition was as black as the oil he periodically drained from the huge motors in his charge. Like Nobbie and Pastor Wondercheck, Pap was mean; indeed, he reveled in his meanness.

Before the pretty Polish girl came to work at Jakub Dworak's Kosher Delicatessen, Nobbie ate his lunch elsewhere but since her arrival had become a regular, often remaining after he picked up his order to talk *at* her. He stood too close during the one-sided exchanges, gestured too flamboyantly, and brayed like a donkey when he laughed. She never responded, keeping her eyes down, her shoulders rolled forward. "He talks too much," Riley once told her after Nobbie was gone. Her aunt had translated, and when the Polish girl smiled at him he'd felt his face redden.

"'O'er the ramparts we watched,'" Jenny Doyle sang as Riley shouldered his way closer to the stage, pushing through a jungle of sharp elbows and peeved expressions. He kept one hand on the pistol in the pocket of his coat. The time was nearing and he was still too far away.

It's not my fault. She sent me to the wrong place!

ANTONI

"A man who shakes his fist can overturn a boat even in calm water," Antoni Pietkowski's father had advised his four sons when they were boys. That was before Sobibor where Jan was worked to death and Filip shot by a guard for sport; before the White Death in his immaculate linen coat watched from the low porch of his bivouac as Father and Szymon filed past in an unbroken line that led to the chambers. The Nazi hauptsturmführer had smoked a cigarette and made a joke as Antoni's father and last surviving brother trudged to their deaths like sheep destined to become lamb chops rather than smoke and ashes. For Antoni, the uprising had taken hold that day, an infant growing to manhood long after the White Death was replaced by Reichleitner and the hated Untersturmführer Nieman.

He sat in the guardroom just outside the cellblock, the radio tuned to the Armed Forces channel. A girl was singing the national anthem of the United States of America.

"'Whose broad stripes and bright stars...'"

Antoni had resisted the trip from Nuremberg to Linz to assist in the interrogation of Franz Stangl. "I'd prefer not," he told the major after learning the identity of the prisoner who would require his services as a translator. The American officer had been surprised.

"I would think you'd want a crack at him, Antoni. Don't you want to see the look on his face when you walk in?"

"I doubt he'll admit he knew me. It's beneath him."

"You never know. A familiar face might loosen his lips…

Make him believe he can talk his way out of a noose by giving up some of the others."

The first interrogation had gone exactly as Antoni predicted, the White Death refusing to look at either man as he sat on his low bunk, wearing green prison fatigues bereft of the medals and emblems once adorning his SS uniform. "I believe you and Mister Pietkowski are already acquainted," the major began after they entered the cell. Stangl had denied it. "Ich kenne inh nicht," he'd muttered without looking up. *I don't know him.* It was a lie. Three years earlier, Stangl had plucked Antoni from among the new arrivals stumbling off the cattle cars used to transport Jews from Warsaw to Sobibor, installing him as his camp interpreter after overhearing the young man converse with guards and inmates in several languages. It had put the young linguistics professor in a line headed for the barracks along with those who had craftsmen's work skills or appeared hale enough to survive the hard labor they would be forced to perform until starvation and brutality made them no longer hale. A second line had formed that day as well, its members taken directly to Lager III, the extermination area.

"'...through the perilous fight,'" the girl on the radio continued, joined by a familiar voice that added subtext in low dignified tones. The famous journalist, Farley Sackstead, spoke of the approaching moment when the nightmare would be over, a measure of finality in his voice that belied reality for Antoni. Some of the monsters who had administered the Holocaust would die on the scaffold, others languishing in prison. But he knew that many would be hired to administer the peace because they'd made the trains run on time. Even more would go home. And they would have homes. Battle-weary foot soldiers and German civilians might have to dig out from under bombed buildings, scrounge for food and shelter, and follow the edicts of new masters, but the land they'd called home before the war would still be home to them.

Not for us.

Warsaw had always been home to Antoni. Born and raised

in the Polish capital city, he and Gosia had married, believing they'd raise a family there. Now they were homeless, hoping to become Americans. Gosia was already in the United States, Antoni to join her once the interrogations and trials were over. He still wasn't sure they'd made the right decision. After accepting the major's offer of a job for him and a visa for Gosia, they'd been approached by Zionists. "We'll need men like you to help establish a Jewish state in Palestine," they'd proposed, citing his command of languages. Antoni had been tempted. Not Gosia. "No matter what they say, Antoni, it's not an interpreter they want," she'd insisted. "They're looking for soldiers. They want you to kill for them, to die for them. I don't want you to die. I want a husband and our child will want a father…not a martyr."

Antoni had spurned the Zionists' efforts to recruit him but now regretted it, his nights wracked with loneliness. He and his wife could have been together in Palestine. Instead, she was in America while he translated questions the major posed to unrepentant men whose Third Reich had destroyed most of both Antoni's family and Gosia's.

"Should we take another crack at him?" the major asked. Antoni looked up from his seat on a bench in the stockade's guardroom The major stood in the open doorway connecting the guardroom to the cellblock.

Antoni shrugged. "I don't see any point, Major. Stangl won't give us anything…especially with a Jew in the room."

The major nodded. An affable man when Nazis weren't in his sights, he continued. "Have you heard from Gosia? She's got to be close to delivery. That must feel good…to be a father. And your baby will be an American. That must feel good too."

It was true, Antoni conceded. Their child would be an American, grow up in the land of milk and honey, have children and grandchildren who would know all the words to the song now being broadcast across the world. It was what he and Gosia had both wanted and yet, as the girl on the radio sang the national anthem of his soon-to-be adoptive country, he no longer found it comforting.

2

7 May 1945

1759:11 to 1759:20 Eastern Standard Time
2359:11 to 2359:20 Central European Time

Farley

"'...we watched were so,'" the girl sang as Farley listened from the glass booth the network had set up in Times Square. It was positioned on the right wing of a temporary stage erected in front of the Landmark skyscraper on closed-off West Forty-Second Street, giving Farley an excellent view of the crowd that stretched from Seventh Avenue to Broadway and then south to Forty-First. Just days earlier, after six years based in London and nearly twenty in Europe, he'd wangled a seat on a cargo plane heading stateside with a layover in Greenland. It had landed at Mitchel Field on the Hempstead Plains of Long Island and he'd caught a ride to Manhattan with a US Army quartermaster who regaled him with stories of his black-market escapades.

"Once Patton's Third Army put the Germans on the run, them Krauts left all kinds o' stuff behind...pistols, flags, field knives, and what-have-you," the opportunistic fellow bragged. "Just let 'em drop along with their dead. Them bodies were treasure troves...watches, rings, and so forth. They left vehicles too. I traded a case o' scotch for a Mercedes-Benz that belonged to a genuine German field marshal. Mint condition 'cept for a shattered windshield and some bloodstains on the front seat. Made me five grand minus another case o' scotch I gave a C-47 pilot to take it back to the States."

Farley had listened without comment, biting his tongue lest he share his disapproval of someone who had so joyfully embraced commerce while others lost their lives in combat. That night the veteran journalist slept in the same bed as his wife, Marta, for the first time in five years, retiring at eight p.m., then waking in the middle of the night. Marta found him in the living room of their apartment, staring out the window. "I'm still on London time," he'd explained. Marta had remained up with him, discussing the future. "Take time off to write a book," she'd suggested. "You have a unique perspective. You were there during the Nazis' rise to power. You knew Hitler before the war." Farley didn't disagree. He did have a unique perspective, reporting on the frighteningly rapid ascendence of German National Socialists between the party's disappointing performance in the 1929 Bundestag elections and the 1933 inauguration of Adolf Hitler as the nation's chancellor and most powerful political figure.

"'...gallantly streaming. And the...'" the girl with the reddish hair and freckles sang, reclaiming Farley's attention as he watched her through the glass of the broadcast booth. Her rendition of the national anthem would be over in less than a minute, marking the beginning of the end of his tenure at CBS radio. He would sign off shortly thereafter, ending a twelve-year marriage that began after the network plucked him from the arms of the *Chicago Tribune* in 1933. "Things are happening in Germany and you know the country better than anyone," the head of the network had asserted, offering Farley five times the money and one thousand-fold the exposure. Farley believed important news usually found its way to people regardless of which outlet brought it to light. He didn't care about the catchment area for his words beyond its inherent value in putting food on the table. But radio had given him an opportunity to end his connection to the *Tribune's* acerbic Bob McCormick, a long, mutually beneficial relationship he'd appreciated but not enjoyed.

In 1926, fresh out of Grinnell College, Farley had pitched his services to the editor of the self-proclaimed "American paper for Americans," contending in a letter to McCormick that a fresh point of view from a member of the young generation was needed on the *Tribune*'s foreign desk. There was no response, and Farley next visited the venerable publication's newly built tower on Michigan Avenue in Chicago, walking directly into McCormick's office. He was promptly escorted out by security and camped near the building's entrance for two full weeks, pestering McCormick each time he entered or exited. The famously prickly newspaperman finally caved in. "All right, goddammit! Get yourself across the pond at your own expense and you can file stories with the London desk. We'll pay five dollars for copy and two dollars for a photo…*if* we publish."

"And I'll get a byline?"

"Don't push it."

It was their last in-person exchange. Over the years, Farley went on to file hundreds of stories and photos while never revisiting Chicago. He became the most famous foreign correspondent in the world, his rate per news item climbing, although McCormick refused to offer official employment until Farley's interview of the dour, newly elected Chancellor of Germany. McCormick sent a telegram the same day the interview went to press. A taciturn man, his message was equally curt:

$3600/year with expense account.

Offer rescinded in 72 hours.

Farley received the telegram while lunching at the Halcyon Hotel in London with the head of CBS news. "We can beat that offer…and then some," the urbane fellow promised.

"I'd have taken less," Farley confessed after signing a contract with the network.

In the crowd outside his booth Farley saw a young man with black hair and heavily lidded eyes try to shove his way past a burly fellow who'd elbowed his own way to the front row by separating a uniformed Marine with ulterior motives from a woman whose hair was piled atop her head like a basket. The black-haired young man's lip was pulled upward at the center, giving him a cat-like face. He seemed nervous, eyes darting back and forth from the singer at center stage to Farley's broadcast booth. A moment later the annoying young engineer knocked on the window that separated their cubicles. Farley looked to the sound. The hastily scrawled message—NOBBIE WANTS COMMENTARY—was again pressed against the other side of the glass. Farley shook his head, scribbling on the back of his own script notes and then holding up the message for the engineer to read as the girl at the microphone sang of "rockets' red glare."

TELL NOBBIE TO GO SCREW HIMSELF!

SELMA

"Sidney! Roger! Caroline!" Selma scolded after three cats upended an open bag of flour on the kitchen counter, scattering white dust and cockroaches in all directions. In the beginning Selma had given her cats names and remembered each. Then six became twelve, twelve became twenty-four, and twenty-four expanded to a hungry mob, shrilly meowing for food or attention or for the sheer joy of shrill meowing. Now she called all the male cats Sidney or Roger, all the females Caroline.

"'...we watched were so gallantly streaming,'" the girl on the radio sang.

Selma remembered the lyrics to "The Star-Spangled Banner" from her school days, she and her classmates standing at Monday morning assembly with hands over their hearts, delivering the words as if indifferently conjugating verbs in Latin class by rote.

Rockets' red glare, the bombs bursting in air... That's next.

Selma hadn't forgotten a bursting bomb of her own, a sizzle of fire that exploded from Carl's console radio on the night of the thunder and lightning. The Voice's words had preceded the bolt of electricity that shot across the room and ignited her husband's Barcalounger, the attendant shock wave knocking her unconscious. After she woke up in the emergency room at Bellevue Hospital, the Voice had called out to her for the first time.

Doctor Goldstein, extension seven... Extension seven, Doctor Goldstein.

It had continued on and on through that night—a litany of

demons called forth until Selma slipped out of the hospital to escape them, wearing an open-backed gown and a pair of thin-soled slippers. She'd returned to her house on East Fifty-Second Street to find the radio destroyed and her deceased husband's padded chair turned into a blackened collection of springs and charred wood. It was still in her living room—Carl's beloved Barcalounger—its cushions now ashes. She'd left it there as a reminder of the Voice's power.

The rest of Carl's things had not been similarly memorialized. Packed up and sold to the Salvation Army's second-hand shop on West Fourteenth Street, the remaining evidence of Carl's life on Earth had been exchanged for twenty dollars and a Philco Model 91 radio shaped like a cathedral. The first voice on the Philco after ensconcing it on a kitchen chair moved into the living room had belonged to Reverend Woodrow Dodge, his nasal tenor in praise of the Almighty soaring to the heavens and then sweeping downward to sonorous lows.

"John tells us, 'Beloved, I wish above all things that thou mayest prosper,'" the reverend had intoned. "Brothers and Sisters, I wish you all to be free of want. And that's why I offer…at no charge whatsoever…the Miracle Holy Water. Listen to proof of its miraculous powers."

"I received the Miracle Holy Water," an emotional woman had then claimed, her voice tremulous. "And three days later a check arrived in the mail for one hundred two dollars and fourteen cents. One hundred two dollars!"

"And fourteen cents!" Reverend Dodge reminded his listeners.

"And fourteen cents!" the woman echoed, sobbing.

"Praise God! One hundred two dollars and fourteen cents!"

"Praise God! Praise Jesus!"

More testimonials had followed, the witnesses working hard to out-blubber one another. Once the last of them had phlegmatically testified, Reverend Dodge repeated his promise, assuring his audience that Miracle Holy Water, save modest shipping and handling charges, was free. Subsequently Selma had submitted her first order, a few days later receiving a tiny vial of Miracle Holy Water, a prayer card, and a re-order form. Over the next several months she faithfully listened to more testimonials and sent more money, a deluge of cash directed into the reverend's pocket in exchange for a trickle of consecrated liquid. True to his word, Reverend Woodrow Dodge had yet to charge Selma a penny for the signature product of his ministry, although she'd been shipped and handled for a good deal more than one hundred two dollars and fourteen cents. She still had faith. "I will be rewarded," she told Riley, the boy who swept floors and washed windows at the delicatessen. "My prayer will be answered…and you will help."

Selma went to the front room, a mob of cats chasing after her as kibble fell through a hole in the pocket of her housecoat. She reached the front window and pulled the curtain back far enough to look out. To the right was the CBS building, the Times Square singer's rendition of "The Star-Spangled Banner" blaring from speakers mounted on its exterior. To the left, separated from CBS headquarters by a parking lot, was the building she'd inherited by default, her parents disowning her in spirit without legally accomplishing it via a final will and testament. A delicatessen now operated where her father's shoe store had once been, rent from the concern and apartments on the upper floors providing Selma with a living. A window on the second floor was open, the curtains pulled aside. The Jew's wife, Mrs. Dworak, was framed in the window, looking back into the room. Behind her the Polish girl who'd arrived a couple of months earlier lay on her back near the foot of the bed. Selma had been spying on her all day, the young woman pushing to deliver her baby for more than an hour now.

That's too long.

Selma turned back to face the room as the girl on the radio sang of rockets' red glare. Forty seconds remained until the end of the war in Europe and the completion of Riley's mission. She glanced down. A round-topped side table sat next to the blackened corpse of Carl's Barcalounger. Erose patches of semi-stained wood marred its surface, the blisters created after heat from the burning chair bubbled varnish that was later peeled off by curious cats. Two books were atop the table: a Bible and a book with rings on its cover marking spots where Carl's condensation-coated beer bottles had washed dye from the brown leather. Memories were rare and unreliable when they came, but Selma remembered. The volume was hers, bought from the bookstore at City College.

I was there.

She squinted and the title came into focus long enough for her to read it.

MERCK MANUAL OF PHYSICAL EXAMINATION

Jenny

Jenny understood why her country had chosen "The Star-Spangled Banner" as its anthem. Nevertheless, she thought the forced marriage of music to lyrics had resulted in something non-melodious and stupid. Worse yet, Francis Scott Key's lyrics spoke of pride and glory and Jenny had seen the newsreels about the war. She'd read Jimmy's letters. War might be prideful, but it wasn't glorious. It was bloody.

At first full of pepper and brag, her brother's missives had turned defensively pedestrian since his deployment two years previous, ignoring reports about his dangerous bombing missions in favor of details about a meal he'd eaten or an unexpectedly good nap. It was as if he wanted to hide the truth from his family, preferring them to view the conflict through the filter of inspiring and sanitized movies like *Mrs. Miniver* or *Back to Bataan*.

"'...were so gallantly streaming,'" Jenny sang on, forcing herself to focus. She'd practiced until the lyrics were as much a part of her as her reddish hair and blue eyes; indeed, she'd not thought it possible to forget them until her high school assembly two days earlier. Jenny had sung before her classmates and teachers many times: talent shows, choir performances, school productions. She no longer had nerves beforehand, and when Principal Weissman called her name, she'd confidently stepped to the microphone and begun, the words coming as if from a teletype—relentless and mechanical. She'd not thought about them, instead focusing on different faces in the audience as if she sang directly to them. It was a performance trick that worked for her just as it should until one of the upturned faces in the school's theater had inexplicably been Jimmy's, his wavy black hair and amiable grin making her stumble on the lyric even though he was four thousand miles away and the face she saw was the annoying Riordan boy who thought himself *so* funny. Startled, she'd lost all the words after that, her classmates surprised at first, and then amused—the titters turning into laughter until Principal Weissman moved across the stage and whispered in her ear.

"Start over."

And Jenny had. She'd started over, ignoring the laughter and catcalls, calling forth the acting skills Mrs. Petroff taught the young thespians in the drama club. Her voice had grown louder and stronger, her patriotism more convincing, and at the coda, no one was laughing. Tears streamed down the cheeks of the girls, the boys gulping back their own as they stood with hands over their hearts. After her final note faded into a few moments of reverent silence, they'd roared with applause that came at Jenny in waves, making her own eyes blurry with tears. Following the assembly Mrs. Petroff had cornered her in the hallway on Jenny's way to American history class. "Always focus, Jenny," she'd reminded her star pupil. "Lyrics are unforgiving. If you give up on them in the middle, they run back to the starting line and wait for you to begin again."

Jenny studied the Times Square crowd as she sang, searching for a receptive face. There were a lot of them. Jostling and carousing with one another at the beginning, most in the audience had settled, their eyes on her. Many of the men and women in uniform stood at attention. Others wept as the reality of the approaching moment took hold. There was still a war in the Pacific but for these New Yorkers the conflict in Europe had always been closer and more real. And so much had been given to win it. Sacrifice had become a way of life—people at their best in a time when things were at their worst. It made the throng assembled at the intersection of Seventh Avenue, Forty-Second Street, and Broadway feel noble, because they had, for the most part, behaved nobly over the last four years, the "dog eat dog" mantra New Yorkers embraced before the war replaced by "all for one and one for all."

Jenny looked for her father among the faces. He was out there, she knew. He'd promised, and ever since Jimmy left for Europe, he'd kept his promises, no longer stumbling home from O'Brien's after midnight with Jameson and Guinness on his breath. Long-faced with a somewhat veiny and bulbous nose—the latter a consequence of Irish blood and whiskey—Dad no longer missed work and he stayed home at night, listening to his console radio with a photo of his uniformed son on the end table next to his ancient, padded easy chair.

There was movement near the front edge of the stage and Jenny's father suddenly appeared, pushing his way between a beautiful woman with a mound of pinned-up blond hair and a soldier who frowned mightily when his elbow lost contact with the woman's breast. Dad wore his company shirt—blue with his name stitched over the breast pocket. Khaki suspenders held up his workpants. He was freshly shaven and Jenny could almost smell the Old Spice aftershave. After he slapped it on, his cheeks were always rosy for a few minutes before turning sallow. "It's his liver," the doctor had reported as if imposing a death sentence, a recollection that made Jenny pause in her performance—merely a fraction of a second most wouldn't notice.

Focus, she cautioned herself as clocks all around the world approached the top of the hour. *Lyrics are unforgiving.*

STANGL

In the beginning, the eyes behind the fences had pleaded for mercy, later burning with accusation; indeed, perhaps contempt.

It was as if they could lift his executioner's cowl, exposing what Stangl subconsciously feared was beneath it: a man not glorious but ordinary. *How many are still alive?* he wondered as the nettlesome sound of America's national anthem blared from the guards' radio. Once numbers in the camp ledger, survivors would be witnesses at his tribunal, their fingers pointed at him like avenging angels. And he would face them alone. The Führer was dead, Goebbels as well, the little weasel murdering his own children before he and his wife committed suicide. Who would be left to tell the truth, Stangl wondered—to take responsibility for commands issued to men who had sworn an oath to follow those orders without question?

I am a soldier. I did my duty. I'm innocent.

Catholic Bishop Hudal understood and had vowed to help him reach a safe haven in South America. But then Stangl was betrayed. He'd been at the bus stop on time and worn the dreary, poorly tailored gray suit Hudal's man had provided, blending in with the others waiting on the sidewalk: fellow Germans with the faces of beaten dogs, their clothes patched and in need of laundering. The bus had arrived as scheduled, but the Americans' truck had raced up and screeched to a halt before he could board, armed soldiers pouring from the vehicle like cockroaches. They'd ignored the others, making straight for him.

How did they know it was me?

Stangl smiled in the darkness of his cell. Even without his trademark white linen coat and Luger with its custom-made silencer extending through a hole he'd cut in his holster, his stature above normal human beings was apparent.

Of course they knew! How could they not?

"'...we watched were so gallantly streaming,'" the girl on the radio sang as eyes appeared in the observation slit of his cell door. Stangl sat up on the edge of the bunk.

"Was willst du?" he growled. *What do you want?*

"Jist makin' sure you ain't offed yerself. Seems to be an epidemic o' that with you Krauts," the voice behind the eyes replied.

Stangl didn't speak English beyond a few words: hello, goodbye, I surrender. He didn't understand what the guard had said, but knew it was a taunt. The American jailers at this stockade were all alike, making him the butt of their jokes and very much impressed with their own wit if raucous laughter was any measure. Stangl thought them to be buffoons, but he was grateful they'd taken him nevertheless. The Russians were barbarians. They'd have beaten him and then shipped him off to a labor camp in Siberia.

I'd rather be killed.

The first interrogation was over. Predictably innocuous, given the American major's pathetic adherence to the rules of the Geneva convention, Stangl had been momentarily unnerved when Antoni entered his cell with the officer. The thumbstrap on the American's holster had been unsecured. Antoni could easily have snatched the sidearm and shot the man who'd forced him to watch as his wife was bedded. The image of Gosia with her full breasts and warm thighs pushed their way into Stangl's thoughts.

Is she still alive?

He hoped so. He loved her; indeed, she was the only woman he'd ever truly loved. Theresa was his wife, but he'd married her only because Hitler favored family men when promotions were considered. Like most of Stangl's career decisions, marriage had been a prudent one. Theresa had been serviceable at social functions and supplied him with three daughters—blond-haired, pink-cheeked props who'd satisfactorily confirmed their father's Aryan purity. He'd gotten his promotions. But since his capture, images of his wife and daughters hadn't filled the empty daytime hours nor his dreams at night. It was Gosia's face he conjured in the darkness of his cell.

He wondered if the worm, Reichleitner, had assumed his place between Gosia's legs. The memory of his replacement as commandant of Sobibor made Stangl sniff with disdain. *Reichleitner! That incompetent faggot wouldn't know what to do with a specimen like Gosia. I should have exterminated her before leaving. It would have been kinder.*

"You hear that there song, Otto?" the guard taunted, speaking through the view slit in the cell door. "Want I should turn up the radio?"

"Nicht Otto, du arschloch!" *Not Otto, you asshole!*

The guard laughed. "Und mein name nicht arschloch."

"Du spricht Deustch?"

"Meine mutter ist Deutstch…and my name ain't asshole. Call me that again and I'll come in there and box yer goddamned Kraut ears. Savvy that? You speak that much English, dontcha?"

"Fick dich," Stangl muttered.

"Yeah, fuck yerself right back."

The eyes remained in the door slit, but Stangl looked away as the girl's voice continued to echo down the cellblock corridor from the radio in the guardroom.

"'and the rockets' red glare…'"

He wondered if Hudal was working to secure his release… or plan his escape. He hoped for the latter and that the arschloch guard would be on duty when it happened. He would force him to his knees, make him beg for his worthless life, then put a bullet between his eyes.

"Fick dich, Joe DiMaggio," he murmured, lifting half-lidded eyes until they met the ones peering at him through the view slit of his cell door. "Fick dich."

Jimmy

Jimmy's crewmates hadn't been happy with him when their deployments were extended. And it *had* been Jimmy's fault, although the youngest member of the *Daisy Mae*'s crew had no way to know what would happen when he raised his hand at the briefing. Most of the B-17 Flying Fortress and B-24 Liberator crews were waiting to be shipped stateside and then separated from the Air Corps. With no bombing missions to fly, their crews hung around the barracks playing cards, shooting baskets on the makeshift court set up on one of the tarmacs, or venturing into nearby Nuremberg to sample coppery German beer and desperate German women. But at the briefing they'd asked about people with photography experience. Jimmy had taken pictures for the student paper at John Adams High in Queens. He'd innocently raised his hand along with a few others, thinking they'd use his skills to take photos of the air crews and their planes for posterity. Instead, it put the *Daisy Mae* and its crew on a list of B-17s assigned to the cryptic Project Casey Jones.

"That's a fella in a baseball poem," Cap whispered when the operation's name was revealed at a later briefing. "Why the heck're they callin' it *that?*" It wasn't unusual for the *Daisy Mae*'s captain to ask his belly gunner for explanations. "You're the smart one in this crew, Jimmy. They shoulda made you captain," Cap often joked even though both knew it wasn't true. The West Virginian had learned to pilot a plane at fifteen and dropped out of high school at sixteen to courier mail and passengers around the Appalachians—taking off from cliff edges, skirting snow-capped peaks, and landing in mountain meadows. He had eagle's vision, an iron backbone, and nerves of steel. With ack-ack popping all around, German fighters swarming about like angry gnats, and other Flying Fortresses plunging earthward in flames, the captain had never wavered, his hand relentlessly steady on the controls, his voice even steadier in their headsets.

"Don't worry, boys. Keep yer eyes peeled and yer ballsacks high. I'll get ya home."

And he'd kept his word. After forty-six bombing runs, the *Daisy Mae*'s crew was intact, waist gunner Waring Krivanek from Nebraska the lone Purple Heart winner, the medal coming after he nearly lost a thumb, trying to unjam his waistgun.

Despite his initial apprehension Jimmy now enjoyed the Casey Jones missions. Without anti-aircraft fire or German fighters to worry about, he could relax and appreciate the rumpled earth far below and the pillowy ocean of clouds when they flew above the weather. They went to different places every day, mostly south. With the *Daisy Mae*'s fuel capacity of 1850 gallons they could stay aloft for up to eight hours, depending on the wind direction, and flew day missions to different parts of

Europe. Twice they had trips with layovers: Hassani airfield in Greece on their way home from the Middle East and a second time at Comiso in Italy after flying over North Africa. Regardless of destination, secrecy surrounded each flight, the crew never knowing they'd reached the appointed place until the captain's voice came through their earpieces.

"Target in ten."

"Roger that, Cap," Jimmy always responded, counting down to zero and then pushing a shutter button, the automatic camera that replaced his twin fifties making a sound like a tiny machine gun as it clicked through its film roll.

"'…were so gallantly streaming.'"

Jimmy wondered what it was like in Times Square. Maeve was probably there…with someone else. Even before her letters stopped, he'd known there was a someone else. At first plaintive with love, her missives gradually took on a tone of obligation rather than affection, no longer recalling their last night together or how much she missed him and instead reporting on the status of her Victory Garden or the latest picture at the Rivoli. Eventually "All my love, Maeve" became "Fondly, Maeve" and then just "Maeve." Jimmy had known others who received "Dear John" letters from their sweethearts, often cuckolded by some flat-footed 4-F working in a defense plant. Jimmy hadn't received such a letter, the fragile love and well-intentioned promises he'd shared with Maeve simply evaporating.

As Jenny's voice resounded from the camp speakers he began to sing along, recalling Yankee games where he'd shouted made-up lyrics just to aggravate their father.

"While we stand here and wait for the ball game to start…"

"Dad's moving a little slow these days," Jenny had written in her last letter, and Jimmy knew that "a little slow" was ominous. "How's Siobhan?" people had asked when Jimmy's mother stopped attending services at St. Barnabas. "She's moving a little slow these days," Dad had answered for the last months of her life. Sharp-witted and feisty before her heart gave out, Siobhan Doyle was simply exhausted at the end. Dad's heart was strong, Jimmy knew. It was drink that would take him even though the big Irishman had stopped imbibing when his son was deployed to Europe with the U.S. Army Air Corps, making a deal with God to give up his nightly liter of Jameson if the Almighty would keep his son safe. God had kept his part of the bargain but taken Brian Doyle's liver as payment, the subtle yellowing of the pipe fitter's sclerae apparent even before his son shipped out.

"'and the rockets' red glare...'" Jenny sang as Jimmy softly sang along with her, the spotlights atop the fence that surrounded Feucht Airfield not yet visible, although their reach had turned darkness into haze on the road ahead.

Gosia

Aunt Ewa and Uncle Jakub had been the only Dworaks prescient enough to leave before the Nazis made it impossible. "We must go, brother," Jakub urged Gosia's father after England and France betrayed Czechoslovakia long before the Nazi invasion of Poland. "It is only a matter of time before the Germans are at our doors." His brother, Gosia's father, was the eldest and head of the family. He'd refused to listen. "Nonsense, Jakub," he'd insisted. "Hitler only wants the Sudentenland. It should be Germany's. It's full of Germans. He has no reason to attack Poland." One year later, long after Uncle Jakub and Aunt Ewa had relocated to America, Nazi tanks and troops stormed across the border and into the Polish frontier. The Dworaks and their neighbors, the Pietkowskis, were rounded up and dispatched, first to the Warsaw ghetto, then to the camps. Childhood sweethearts Antoni Pietkowski and Gosia Dworak had been married for only a few months.

"'we watched were so...'" the girl on the radio sang as Aunt Ewa asked the midwife a question, worry clouding her features.

"You make opening bigger?"

"I already told you. That's not the issue. The baby is facing the wrong way. And your niece's pelvis is too narrow."

"Feet are down?"

The midwife, Rita, sighed noisily. "No...as I've already *told* you, the head is down but the face is turned the wrong way. It's called occipital posterior. Makes it harder for the baby to come out. Plus, her ischial spines are narrow. That doesn't help."

"We get doctor...a hospital?"

"She can push it out if you'll quit babying her," Rita sniffed. "She needs to stop making noise and push harder."

Ewa Dworak was a tiny woman, barely five feet tall, and ferocious when ferocity was required. However, Gosia needed this bitch of a midwife and Ewa knew it. So she nodded, murmuring in Polish.

"Suka." *Bitch.*

"What does that mean," Rita demanded. "Suka?"

"Means 'push.'"

"Push?"

"Yes...ty peiprzono suka." *You fucking bitch.*

"What's that one... Push hard?"

"Yes... Ty peiprzono suka... Push hard."

"'...gallantly streaming,'" the girl on the radio sang as Gosia and her aunt flashed tiny smiles at each other. It was a rare moment of amusement in a day otherwise not at all amusing. Gosia had awakened early in the morning to a giant wet spot on the bedsheets, the contractions starting soon thereafter. She'd tried to reach Antoni—to tell her husband that he would be a father by day's end—but the transatlantic cable had been flooded with calls and she was repeatedly rebuffed by the long-distance operators, eventually giving up when the contractions became too intense. Now, with her labor in its twelfth hour and her aunt's worry deafening despite the little woman's soft voice, Gosia despaired. She felt trapped—as if she were once again aboard the packed, fetid railcar as it pulled into the death camp at Sobibor.

The train had wheezed to a stop that day alongside a series of ramps, the prisoners herded out with the guards blowing whistles as they directed inmates into one of two lines. Gosia and Antoni had been immediately pulled apart by a stout prison matron who obviously hated pretty Jewish girls. Reeking of cabbage and envy, she'd shoved Gosia into the line headed for Lager III: the extermination area. That would have been the end of her but for Antoni. Already designated the camp interpreter after Stangl heard him speak to the other prisoners in several languages, he'd cautiously suggested that a man of the commandant's importance warranted a private maid. He'd recommended Gosia, knowing his beautiful wife's duties would not be confined to scrubbing and dusting. Later he'd apologized, tears trailing down his cheeks.

"Forgive me, my sweet Gosia, but it was the only way. You understand, don't you? The only way."

Stangl had soon realized that there was little need for Antoni's language skills. The majority of Sobibor's new arrivals went directly to the extermination area while those kept alive to work in Lagers I and II spoke German or quickly picked up enough of the language to stay out of Lager III. Nevertheless, Stangl kept Antoni close, forcing him to watch when he rutted about atop Gosia, gagging her with his sauerkraut breath and cheap cologne, his swollen member deep inside her. He was large in that way and proud of it. "Have you ever had such a man as I?" he repeatedly asked when they lay in bed afterward, his boast as much for his translator as Gosia. "Never," Gosia always answered, knowing Stangl would beat her or perhaps kill Antoni if she denied it. Besides, it was true. The SS officer's penis was truly huge, although size was all he could crow about in the bedroom. A terrible lover, he was awkward and insecure, slapping her if the moans she manufactured were unconvincing, then wheedling for praise. He was so unlike Antoni. Gosia's husband hadn't known other women before her, yet he'd been instinctively skilled on their wedding night—gentle and yet assertive, patient and attentive—far more of a man than Stangl despite the horse's cock that dangled between the commandant's legs.

The girl on the radio continued to sing as Gosia prayed for her next contraction to push Stangl from her mind and the stubborn baby from her womb.

"'...and the rockets' red glare...'"

She felt tension in her abdomen, drew in a deep breath and held it, then began to push. Aunt Ewa stopped her.

"Jeszcze nie kochanie," she said. "Jeszcze nie." *Not yet, dear... Not yet.*

ZIMMER

"'...we watched were...'" the singer's voice flowed into the night from the Feucht Airfield loudspeakers. Zimmer spoke no English. He didn't understand the words. But he recognized the melody. It had played twenty-four times at the 1936 Olympics in Berlin, not sung *a cappella* like the distant female performer but an instrumental recording with horns and drums. Zimmer had attended several events during the two-weeks-long festival, including all four gold-medal performances by the celebrated American sprinter, Jesse Owens. Although Hitler had been a mainstay for much of the games, shaking hands and posing for photographs with German athletes, he'd not attended Owens's award ceremonies, an absence Zimmer had welcomed. Without an ominous cloud of disapproval from the Führer hovering above the stadium, he and his fellow spectators had embraced the Olympic ideal of global harmony, enthusiastically applauding the remarkable Black American. The feeling was short-lived. Three years later the promise of a world at peace was shattered when Zimmer and his fellow soldiers crossed the border into Poland.

The singer's words, delivered in English, reminded the young Wehrmacht soldier that Germany and America might still be at war, and he stepped back into the cover of the forest.

Is it midnight? Is it over?

He remained motionless, eyes sweeping back and forth in search of movement along the road below him. There was none.

I could approach the gates... Surrender tonight. Get something to eat and drink. Perhaps, a shower.

"'...so gallantly streaming.'"

...or I could just go home.

Home was Ingolstadt, the beautiful city where Zimmer had been born and raised; where he'd gone to school and fished and rowed the Danube with his best friend, Karl Janning; where he'd fallen in love with Karl's little sister, Ilse. Originally a fortress city surrounded by a medieval defensive wall, perhaps Ingolstadt was no longer standing. After the Luftwaffe was rendered impotent, the Americans and British had relentlessly bombed German cities, and the Wehrmacht soldier knew his town might be a roofless wasteland of charred walls and shattered glass. He'd received no letters in weeks. His mother and father might be dead, his sisters Greta and Astrid as well. And Ilse. He'd held her last letter high above his head when he and Braun crossed the Pegnitz River, more afraid the ink would run than a bullet would hit him. *Ich warde ewig warten, mein Schatz*, she'd written, and he believed her. She would wait forever. Unless, Zimmer anguished, the dark of her own forever had come, reuniting her with her brother, Karl.

From the cover of the woods Zimmer studied the paved roadway leading to the American air base. It was about two meters below him, a shoulder with high, raggedy grass separating it from a knee-high embankment and then a gentler upward slope to the tree line. About fifty meters from where he stood, the road angled sharply left, the curve dimly illuminated by the natural light of the moon and man-made luminosity from lamps Zimmer presumed had been mounted on the fence surrounding the airfield. With nightfall grounding flights and settling most of the creatures in the forest, it was quiet save the voice of the American singer, coming from speakers on the airbase. She sang with emotion, recalling for Zimmer the early years after Hitler became chancellor—a time when he and Karl stood alongside their fellow Hitlerjugend and sang the German national anthem with innocence and zeal.

"*Deutschland, Deutschland über alles,
Über alles in der Welt...*"

That was before 9 November 1938—the Night of Broken

Glass—when the Führer's thug Brownshirts were unleashed on Jews all across Germany. Both Zimmer's family and Ilse's had Jewish friends and neighbors in Ingolstadt. They'd tried to help, standing in front of Posen's Meat Shop and Dr. Adler's house with its small clinic. Zimmer wore his Hitlerjugend uniform, as had Ilse's brother, Karl, hoping to direct vandals away. It had worked. There were a few scuffles, but they'd saved Herr Posen's store and the clinic. Others were not so fortunate. All across the country, homes and stores were vandalized, people beaten, synagogues torched. Nearly one hundred German Jewish citizens were killed, including the boys' teacher, Herr Viedt—clubbed to death wearing the Iron Cross he'd earned while serving in the Kaiser's army during World War I.

Zimmer and Karl were called up to the Wehrmacht army a few weeks later, mustering into the 76th Division—part of Army Group South under the command of General Gerd von Rundstedt. They'd met Braun—a butcher's son from Berlin— and formed a friendship, the three infantrymen marching with their regiment into Poland against virtually no resistance in September of 1939. Only a handful of their number had been killed during the invasion, one of them a man in Zimmer's platoon who was shot by a farmer wielding a French Berthier carbine from World War I. It was the first death Zimmer and Karl had seen close up and they'd been shocked into inaction, their Mausers remaining strapped to their shoulders, their jaws agape, their eyes widened in horror. Not Braun. After helping his father slaughter more pigs and cattle than he could recall, the butcher's son shot and killed the farmer without flinching. Their platoon leader had then ordered them to burn the farmhouse to the ground, the man's wife and children left alive to watch their home go up in smoke. Zimmer had thrown a torch into the conflagration, a symbolic gesture with the place already engulfed in flames. He'd proudly detailed the incident in a letter to Ilse. Her response had shamed him.

Oh, that poor woman and her children.

"'and the rockets' red glare...'" the girl on the radio sang as Zimmer continued to survey the road to the airfield below him. Empty of traffic at this late hour, it was level and smooth, unpocked by bomb craters.

Go now or wait until morning?

In daylight, Zimmer knew he could approach the guards at the gates with arms held high above his head, his lack of weapons apparent, his desire to surrender unequivocal. At night, a nervous sentry might see a silhouetted figure materialize from the darkness and shoot him. The young soldier's stomach abruptly gurgled as if weighing in. He and Braun had last eaten on Sunday. Today was Monday, now almost Tuesday. He was famished. Zimmer took a step outside the edge of the forest, then abruptly stopped.

Someone was on the road.

Riley

"'…we watched were so gallantly streaming,'" pretty Jenny Doyle sang as Riley edged nearer. After insinuating himself through the crowd, he'd almost reached her, a single line of spectators separating him from the elevated stage on which Jimmy Doyle's sister stood and performed. "She's the nicest person ever," Jimmy had promised him, his words prophetic. Jenny was indeed the nicest person Riley had ever encountered, meeting him at the train station after he was sent home from Fort Benning, then linking her arm in his to lead him through the crowded depot. Her touch had been thrilling, her soft smile and tender heart bewitching him.

He'd spent the night at the Doyles' home in Queens, then returned to Buffalo. Jenny escorted him back to the train station, then politely waited for him to board his train. At the top of the railcar steps he'd hesitated, calling out to her. "I love you, Jenny."

Her eyes had widened with surprise, her lips parting.

"I love you," he'd repeated and she'd hesitated, then lifted a hand to wave goodbye, managing a response as the train began to move.

"Thank you, Riley."

He'd stayed on the steps, gripping a handrail and watching as her figure on the platform grew smaller, then became a dot, then a memory—elated and filled with hope and love because she'd not laughed…or meowed. In Buffalo, he'd gone back to the same pre-war Great Lakes freighter job Pap had arranged for him after the eighth grade didn't work out. Riley had a stoker's rating, a job that kept him below deck most of the time—retrieving tools his father and the other enginemen used to keep the huge motors tuned, swabbing spills and sweeping, or wiping down and polishing whatever he was told to wipe down and polish. Nights, he sweated in his narrow berth until heat and snoring and farts sent him to the main deck where he sat in the forward section below the bridge, watching the stars and dreaming of Jenny Doyle, the distant hum of the engines gently lulling him to sleep.

On his shore leaves he wandered around Buffalo all day, sometimes going to the movies where he watched cowboys battle Indians, cops take down robbers, and handsome men know exactly what to say to beautiful women. At night he lay in his narrow bed as Pap loudly snored in the next room. With Dinah Shore or Helen Forest or Lena Horne on the radio, Riley imagined whirling Jimmy Doyle's sister around a dance floor, pulling her close, grazing her soft bottom with his fingers. He'd told Pap about Jenny, but immediately regretted it. Albert Blaine had roared with laughter.

"No girl in her right mind wants anything to do with an imbecile, Felix."

Imbecile.

It was the same word Pastor Wondercheck had used. Before Mom's disappointment with life's possibilities led to a love affair with sugary sweets and fried foods that tripled her chin and obliterated her waistline, she'd sought advice and comfort from the unctuously handsome clergyman. The pastor had promptly advised and comforted his way into her bed during Pap's long absences on the Lakes. "Play in your room, Riley," Mom told him when the pastor visited. But the walls were thin and the five-year-old had eventually followed Pastor Wondercheck's porcine grunts and Mom's soft moans to the open doorway of her bedroom where he saw the reverend's white buttocks between his mother's widespread legs.

When Riley was fifteen—long after Mom had eaten her way out of Pastor Wondercheck's affections—her gall bladder burst. She died and Riley confronted the minister at the funeral. The pastor shrugged him off.

"It's your imagination, boy. Imbeciles don't have memories."

"I know what that word means. It means stupid. I ain't stupid. I ain't no imbecile. I remember things, and I remember you!"

Jenny continued to sing from the high stage in Times Square as Riley tried to wedge himself between a soldier in uniform and a pretty woman with blond hair piled atop her head.

"'and the rockets' red glare…'"

A large man—his shirt blue, his suspenders khaki, his aftershave Old Spice—beat him to the spot, shoving his way to the front. It blocked Riley's view of Jenny—the suspendered man too wide, the soldier too tall, the blond's mound of hair too high—but he could see the countdown clock at the back of the stage. Perched atop a tower fashioned from iron pipes and held together by thick wire, it had three hands: two fat and one thin. He recalled the Cat Woman's instructions.

"Wait until the fat hands connect the 12 and the 6."

He put a hand in the pocket of his long overcoat. The pistol was still there. "I can shoot," he'd promised the Cat Woman. "In boot, I hit the target ninety times outta one hundred. I passed that test."

The thin hand of the huge clock at the rear of the stage continued to move, describing a relentless, steady arc. Riley wrapped his fingers more tightly around the grip of the gun.

"Wait…until the fat hands connect the 12 and the 6."

Antoni

Just as Antoni anticipated, the first round of Stangl's interrogation had yielded nothing useful, yet the major was reluctant to give up. "I don't think he knows anything," Antoni reiterated to the American officer. "He's too arrogant to keep a secret. He'd want everyone to know that he was in the…"

Antoni paused, searching for the right word. His English was very good but American idioms were elusive.

"In the loop?" the major offered.

"Yes, that's it…in the loop. He'd want everyone to know he was in Hitler's loop."

Through the open door leading to the cellblock Antoni could hear the duty guard. A sergeant, he stood outside Stangl's cell and spoke to the prisoner through the view slit. A career soldier, the guard was very loud with a pronounced drawl distinctive to the American South. He was also a talker, earlier sharing his war record with Antoni while the major conferred with the captain of the guard in another office.

"Spent my whole career in the military police. Never saw a minute o' combat other than bar fights. Then the war come along and I figger here's my chance. Instead, they keep me stateside breakin' up fights 'tween boys on liberty after basic training. I wanted to fight, but when they finally gimme orders to ship out, damned thing was put near over. So here I am… back with the MPs, roundin' up these Nazi boys and keepin' 'em under lock and key. Damned shame. I woulda liked to kill me some Krauts."

Unlike the sergeant, the major spoke with an accent peculiar to upper crust New England, each word delivered as if through clenched teeth. It was the speech pattern of a patrician, but thus far Antoni had found the American officer to be unaffected—a good man although a typical American. Everything was fast. The Americans walked fast, talked fast, made quick decisions, then immediately acted upon them. They lived for the future and discarded the past as if it were an empty bottle. "Your whole life is in front of you, Antoni," the major kept telling him, as if those harrowing and hopeless months in the death camp could be shed like snakeskin. He meant well. But he also slept without Antoni's nightmares: the door battered down, herded into the street with Gosia, the ghetto at Warsaw, the people packed together in cattle cars.

The Pietkowskis had arrived at Sobibor near the start of Stangl's tenure. There were three parts to the camp: Lager I with a bakery as well as tailor, carpentry, mechanical, and sign-painting shops; Lager II where the administration buildings and farm were located; and Lager III, the extermination area. Those who detrained were quickly separated into two queues: one leading to the barracks, the other to Lager III. A husky matron had pulled Gosia away from Antoni and pushed her into the line heading for Lager III. At the same time a fight broke out after a guard grabbed a young woman and began to fondle her breasts. The woman's husband was large, his shoulders broad, his neck thick. He'd attacked the guard and Stangl—the man they came to know as the White Death—strode over while unholstering his side weapon, an odd piece with a long custom-made silencer.

"This is holding up the line," he'd shouted in German, putting the barrel of his gun to the husband's head and then pulling the trigger. Rather than a sharp report, the gun had issued a spitting sound, the husband crumpling to the ground like a stringless marionette. Afterward the White Death shot the woman, too, and the lines resumed moving forward, Gosia taken farther from Antoni with each step.

"Everyone stay in line," Antoni had immediately called out in Polish, repeating the words in Russian, then Hungarian, then German, then French. When the White Death heard him, he'd issued a terse order.

"Bring that one to my quarters."

Inside the commandant's bivouac Antoni had discovered a reception area with a rodent-like aide ensconced behind a desk and a single file cabinet shoved against one wall. A door behind the aide led to Stangl's private quarters, a slightly larger space with enough room for a desk, a narrow bed, a footlocker, and a metal armoire. Stangl had yet to fully unpack, the place messy with clothing, toiletries, and other personal items the hauptsturmführer had strewn about. Perusing a document from behind his desk, the SS officer had spoken to Antoni in German without looking up.

"I need an interpreter. Most of you goddamned Polacks can't speak German and none of the Russians can."

"I understand. Begging your pardon, Herr Hauptsturmführer, but perhaps you will employ a maid? My wife is an excellent housekeeper—"

"Sei ruhig dreckiger Jude!" *Be quiet, filthy Jew!*

Lifting his eyes from the document until they rested on Antoni, Stangl had slowly and deliberately unholstered his weapon, placed it on his desk, and then called out to his aide.

"Kurth!"

By the time the young officer appeared in the doorway separating the commandant's private chamber from the reception area, Stangl's eyes were back on his document.

"This Jew is now the camp interpreter. His wife will be my maid. See to it."

He'd lifted his eyes then, a perverse smile creasing his lips.

"And you might hurry. I don't know which line she has joined."

"'...gallantly streaming,'" the girl on the radio sang, the drawling sergeant's voice competing with hers as he taunted Stangl through the open view slit in the cell door. Stangl had tolerated the guard's jabs until now but suddenly responded, his familiar growl making Antoni involuntarily shudder.

"Fick dich!" *Fuck you!*

The guard responded with his own insult. From habit as a linguist, Antoni echoed his words and drawl in a whisper.

"What did you say to me?"

Antoni looked up. One of the major's eyebrows was raised,

his jaw thrust forward. Antoni suppressed a sigh. Americans were an affable bunch most of the time but quick to get their collars up. They were like Germans in that way; indeed, the GIs he'd met were more like Germans than their English and French allies.

"Nothing, Major," Antoni answered. "Just practicing my English."

The major's face relaxed. "It's very good, Antoni…your English. And you nailed the accent."

3

7 May 1945

1759:21:1759:30 Eastern Standard Time
2359:21 to 2359:30 Central European Time

Farley

The engineer—hair uncombed, shirt untucked, cheeks at least three days past a needed shave—held a different note up to the glass partition, the hastily scrawled lettering a perfect match for his appearance.

Nobbie's coming!!!

Farley shrugged. Nobbie Wainwright—the florid ad man, former sportscaster, and interim producer for the evening's broadcast—might pull him off the air, putting an unceremonious cap on a legendary career, but Farley didn't care. He'd been trained to *report* the story, not *be* the story. It was a lesson imparted by McCormick after Farley's first serious piece made it past the editor at the *Tribune's* London desk. As a stringer he'd filed a number of stories by then, a few earning the agreed-upon five dollars when they made it onto the back pages of the publication. Those were lean days. Based in Vienna and Paris, he'd subsisted on money earned by translating German and French technical journals into English. However, his coverage of the first speech by Adolph Hitler after Germany lifted the ban on the National Socialist Party opened McCormick's eyes. From Vienna, where Farley had met and fallen in love with Marta, he'd traveled to Berlin for Hitler's speech, subsequently both awed and terrified by the future Führer's undeniable charisma.

Four thousand fervent supporters waited inside Berlin's Clou

Concert Hall, the air filled with the sounds, sights, and smells of anticipation. Then Herr Hitler appeared and the crowd became a single living thing, one threatening to digest those not enraptured by the fiery oratory that followed.

There was more, the prose more purple with each sentence. Farley begged the London editor to forward the story to Chicago without change. "Not a good idea, son," the avuncular senior man cautioned him over the telephone, his warning justified by McCormick's telegram the next day.

> YOU'RE A REPORTER, SACKSTEAD, NOT A NOVELIST. WRITE WHO, WHAT, WHEN, WHERE, AND HOW. NO MORE G_____D LITERARY RHETORIC!

The piece ran, absent Farley's grandiloquent prose, with one of the *Tribune's* veteran staffers rewriting it and then claiming the byline. An addendum at the end acknowledged that "This report included contributions from Farley Sackstead." Farley's rate was bumped to ten dollars and he'd immediately proposed to Marta, the daughter of a Viennese diplomat. They married and decided to travel—traversing Italy, hopscotching to Greece, and then taking a steamer to Alexandria. After a crowded train trip to Cairo they were shamed by their provincialism, preconceived notions of Egypt's capital—primarily drawn from Rudolf Valentino movies—challenged by the architecture and sophistication of a modern African city. Farley wrote a piece about it that McCormick approved for the Sunday Travel section, another staffer again polishing and claiming the principal author byline. This time, the *Tribune* publisher gave Farley a credit as the second author, and wired twelve dollars with a message sans an exclamation point:

> BETTER, BUT STILL TOO G_____D LONG.

The newlyweds stayed in Egypt for a month, enjoying open-air cafes and markets, marveling at the antiquities in Cairo's vast Egyptian Museum, strolling Gezira Island's leafy Zamalek district, and enjoying panoramic views of the city from atop the 187 meters-tall Cairo Tower. One day they shared a tour bus to

Giza with a group of children enrolled at the city's American School. There they were awed by the enigmatic engineering of the Pyramids and the Great Sphinx. Marta befriended the young Egyptian woman chaperoning the students. "My husband is an aide to King Fuad's chief advisor. He can arrange for your husband to interview His Majesty," she promised Farley's wife. Farley's subsequent conversation with the prickly Sultan-turned-King was picked up by the international wire services after McCormick ran it on the front page. This time he paid Farley fifty dollars, resisted writing another barbed critique, and gave him an expense account.

"'…the bombs bursting in air,'" the girl in Times Square sang as Farley considered a career of twenty years about to end, perhaps ignominiously if Nobbie Wainwright lived down to his reputation of enraged outbursts and impulsive decisions. Farley was forty-two years old. Still a young man, he could write a book, as Marta had suggested. He glanced at the television monitor on his desk. Although the V-E Day broadcast was on the radio only, CBS had scattered experimental RCA cameras around Times Square. "It's a chance for you to see how many perspectives you can report on while never moving from your chair," CBS network chief Bill Paley promised. Farley was skeptical. The small screen—nine inches on a diagonal—made the vast Times Square gathering seem less impressive than the real thing, as a remote director flicked the grainy images from one screenshot to another.

It was not the famous newsman's first exposure to television production. The day after his arrival in New York, Paley had arranged for him to be in the control room at rival station WNBT during an airing of the drama series *Dr. Death*. "It'll give you an idea of how it works," the head of CBS told him. Farley had subsequently joined the program's director, watching actors on a row of monitors while the messy-haired fellow pointed a finger at one screen and then another, blandly intoning, "One…now three…back to one…now two."

Farley watched the small television screen as the images

shifted: Jenny Doyle at the microphone, the crowd facing her, a view from behind the amassed gathering that made the stage distant. He could picture the director of tonight's closed-circuit production, speaking into the microphone mounted on his control panel.

One...now three...back to one...now two.

On the monitor a previously unused camera angle popped up. Positioned behind Jenny Doyle, it showed the packed gathering from her viewpoint. Farley's reporter's instincts immediately drew him to the young man with dark hair and darker eyes. Stealing glances at the singer over the shoulder of a man in the front row, the boy rose on tiptoes, then retreated behind the burly fellow's broad frame, rose again and then retreated. Farley shifted his gaze from the virtual image on the monitor to an actual view through his booth's glass wall. From the new angle the boy was hidden behind the larger fellow in front and Farley returned his eyes to the TV screen. A moment later he forgot about the dark-eyed young man, instead watching the grainy television images rotate between camera angles as he ruminated on the world's future and his own.

One...now three...back to one...now two.

Selma

"'...the bombs bursting in air,'" the temptress on the radio sang. Somewhere in her increasingly fuzzy memory Selma placed the words in another time and place—a long-ago Fourth of July resounding with cries of "Remember the Maine!" It was 1898. She'd attended the Independence Day parade down Fifth Avenue that year with her friends, wearing a new and very fashionable hat, her long auburn hair spilling out and then cascading to her shoulders. She'd had a drizzle of freckles across the bridge of her nose and she was pretty. She went to private school with children from old New York families, and many of the boys liked her, keeping their distance because she was Carl Filbert's girl—raw-boned, rebellious, public-school Carl who'd loudly vowed to enlist and "go kill Spaniards" by day's end, instead drifting off with his friends to guzzle beers and explode firecrackers. "He's a bum," Father had warned her from the beginning, but Selma insisted she could change him. That was before her brother, Owen, had his last argument with Father and left for good; before the unexpected pregnancy and the day she came home from school and found her things on the sidewalk; before the marriage to Carl and the traumatic miscarriage at seventeen that nearly killed her and left her barren; before her deadbeat husband began to stay out late and come home wearing the scent of other women. Long, long before days became years.

Standing next to Carl's burnt-out chair, Selma could almost feel her late husband's rancorous presence. By the end of his life he rarely left his precious Barcalounger—a sanctuary acquired at the start of the war—abandoning it only to eat, urinate, or loudly vacate his bowels with the bathroom door wide open.

"*Please, close it, Carl!*"

"*Shut up, goddammit! I can't hear the radio!*"

The rear of the CBS building across the parking lot was visible through a split in the ancient dusty curtains that drooped forlornly across the picture window in Selma's living room. Before the special V-E Day broadcast began she'd watched Nobbie Wainwright and his redhead enter the rear door of the building. Their unexpected appearance hadn't been part of her plan and she'd worried Riley might be distracted after he followed them inside, pausing in his mission to spy on their coupling. He was a boy. Boys did such things—yet another reason, besides his dimwittedness, that she didn't like relying on him. But she'd no choice, her blurred vision and erratic tremors rendering her aim unreliable.

I've done all I could!

And she had. Selma had made Riley repeat the instructions until certain he'd not forget; drawn a large *L* on his hand to help him find the studio once he was inside the building; given him Carl's coat with pockets deep enough to hide the weapon; and manufactured the bullets in Carl's old basement workshop.

Resurrecting the Hills Brothers coffee cans still half-filled with hollow brass cartridges, copper noses, cylindrical primers, and ancient gunpowder, she'd carefully followed her dead husband's recipe, producing six bullets dipped in Reverend Woodrow Dodge's Miracle Holy Water. Her plan had seemed foolproof until the Voice subverted her, originating his broadcast from Times Square rather than the CBS studio.

She knew Riley was upset with her for sending him to the third-floor studio instead of Times Square. After leaving the CBS building he'd spotted her face in the opening between the drapes and glowered as he ran across the parking lot. She wasn't worried. She would fill him with Oreos and then take him to the movies. He would get over it.

...or forget.

One car was in the parking lot. It belonged to the man who queued up the pre-recorded mysteries and musical programs set to air after the Voice signed off. Nobbie Wainwright and the redhead were gone. "Nobrains Nobbie," Selma muttered, recalling the day she'd demanded to see the head of the network and a smarty-pants receptionist instead sent her to Nobbie's office. "Cast out the demon Voice," she'd insisted, showering the sportscaster with droplets of Miracle Holy Water. Nobrains was bulky then, bulkier now. He reminded her of Carl, an aura of rage and expectation coating him like a layer of grease. "Get the hell out of my office, you goddamned lunatic!" he'd shouted, afterward grabbing her arm and then shoving her out the door. She'd fallen and hurt her wrist, but he was no gentleman and had done nothing to help her.

A cat rubbed his back against her leg and Selma looked down. It was one of the Rogers. He stood on his back legs and pawed at her until she bent to pick him up. "There's a good kitty... Such a good little kitty," she purred, stroking his fur, her fingers bumping across doughy mats. Her cooing invited a swarm of cats to join them, the suddenly frenetic animals scrambling out from under furniture or racing into the living room from other parts of the house. They surrounded her, rubbing against her legs and sinking claws into her thick wool leggings—morphing into a single undulating thing that serenaded her with insistent caterwauling. "'…gave proof through the night…'" the siren on the radio joined in, her voice suddenly louder as if to taunt Selma. It filled her with unease. Riley was a man—not much of one, to be sure—but man enough to be drawn into the sweet embrace of a Jezebel.

The Roger in her arms rubbed the top of his head on her chin as if to reassure her that she could trust Riley. She relaxed. Of course she could trust him. He was simpleminded but true. He had pledged his love to the girl. He would not betray her with a succubus.

"There's a good kitty," Selma said, stroking the Roger's fur. "There's a good kitty."

Jenny

After Jimmy was deployed Jenny had refused to believe he might not survive, certain God and luck of the Irish would see him through the conflict. That was before the newsreels with images of planes like Jimmy's amidst tiny puffs of anti-aircraft fire. Inspirational and sanitized features followed the newsreels with handsome actors pretending at war or impossibly beautiful actresses impersonating stalwart women on the home front. Jenny remembered only the grainy black-and-white films that preceded them.

Shortly after his arrival in England, Jimmy had sent a photo of the B-17 on which he would be the belly gunner, her brother grinning at the cameraman through the Plexiglas of his underside turret, the photographer just a few feet away. The nightmare for Jenny had begun that night: Jimmy dangling from the bottom of his B-17 bomber, the turret gone, one hand holding tight to a single barrel of the guns he called his "twin fifties." In the recurring dream he called out to Jenny for help, and suddenly she was inside the plane, looking down at him, the roar of the propellers and the mad rush of wind in her ears. She reached out for him. And then he lost his grip and was falling, his face growing smaller, her name on his lips ever more distant until she woke up, sobbing, with Dad calling out from his room down the hall.

"You're dreaming again, Jenny. It's just a dream."

"'…the bombs bursting in air…'" Jenny sang, shuddering as she fought off the image of her brother's death. Many of the faces in the Times Square crowd were now wet with tears. Dad was crying, too, and Jenny suddenly felt her own tears forming. One trickled down her cheek and yet her voice didn't tremble as she wept; indeed, it was stronger and louder, soaring into the night and swelling with pride. She *was* proud that America—her country—had triumphed over the evil Nazis, proud that the fight against tyranny and betrayal would not end until victory in the Pacific was achieved. She was proud of her brave brother who had volunteered rather than wait for conscription; proud of Dad who'd kept his promise to God and stayed sober; proud of those who'd gone to war and those who'd stayed home to help the defense plants churn out tanks and planes and warships; proud of herself for remembering all the lyrics to "The Star-Spangled Banner" and projecting to the audience just as Mrs. Petroff had taught her. Most of all, she was proud to be finishing the damned thing in less than one and a half minutes, a certainty at this midpoint of her performance. She could relax now, find a note to hold a bit longer, put her own mark on the song. *"Find someone in the audience or think of the person you're singing to,"* Mrs. Petroff always told her students. And Jenny did, closing her eyes and visualizing her brother with his familiar gash of a grin, his eyes sparkling with intelligence and mischief.

Other voices rose into the night as many in the audience sang along. From behind, she heard Mayor LaGuardia's reedy tenor as he valiantly joined in, singing relentlessly off-key. Jenny focused on her own voice, tuning out Hizzoner by thinking of her soft-hearted brother and the way he picked up strays: dogs, cats, kids in school who lunched alone or found the corners at dances. Jimmy had picked up another stray in the army: the doleful boy who'd washed out of basic training. *He's a strange kid, sis. He's had a hard time of it here,* Jimmy had written. *He's on his way back to Buffalo with a long layover in New York. He'll need a place to stay for the night. Just feed him and then put him on the couch. Don't ask why he was sent home.*

Not long after her brother's letter, Jenny met his friend at Penn Station. She'd brought a hand-lettered sign with his name, but after the boy detrained—his brow ridged, his eyes dark with bruising, an even darker shadow of GI haircut low on his forehead—he'd glanced at it and then walked on as if the words were written in a foreign language. Jenny had never met him and yet knew from her brother's description that it was his friend. "Riley," she'd called out, the boy turning at the sound of his name.

"Jenny?"

She'd taken him home on the subway, chattering nonstop once she figured out that Riley Blaine wasn't about to chatter at all, instead sneaking glances at her as if she were a precious gem unexpectedly discovered in a mound of simple stones. At dinner he wolfed down the beef stew she'd prepared as her father held forth until his opinions were so strident Jenny frowned him into silence. Riley spent the night on the couch and she'd escorted him back to the train station the next morning. "I love you, Jenny," he'd told her before boarding the 9:00 a.m. to Buffalo. She'd not been surprised, the strange boy's puppy dog eyes betraying him. Nevertheless, she'd not known what to say, eventually managing to awkwardly thank him. "I hope I didn't hurt his feelings," she later told Bridget. Her friend had taken a more jaundiced view. "Just pray he doesn't turn up on your doorstep," she'd replied.

"'...gave proof...through the night,'" Jenny sang, hesitating for a fraction of a beat when a flash of dark eyes appeared over her father's shoulder—there for an instant, then gone.

Riley?

She pressed on, faltering almost imperceptibly when the dark eyes reappeared, then gathering herself and forging ahead with her eyes again closed, visualizing Jimmy as she crossed the song's midfield and headed for the goal line.

Stangl

The American military policeman continued to study his prisoner through the cell's view slit as if Stangl were an animal in a zoo. The SS officer bared his teeth.

"Hast du angst vor dem wolf?" he growled. *Are you afraid of the wolf?*

"Where I'm from, we eat wolves for breakfast," the guard drawled, speaking to his prisoner in German.

Stangl slid back on his bunk until his face was hidden in shadows. The jailer's taunts didn't anger him nor did the American major frighten him; indeed, the only emotion he'd allowed since arriving in Linz was the flicker of surprise on his face when Antoni Pietkowski followed the major into his cell. He'd pretended not to know him and the interrogation had proceeded with Antoni dispassionately translating Stangl's responses to the American major's questions. The major had been frustrated with Stangl, his prisoner offering no useful information because he had none. Stangl had no idea what had become of others who'd served with him in the euthanasia program nor did any of them know what had become of him. "Secrecy is paramount," Hudal had cautioned. "Do not share your plans with others. Do not arrange to meet with friends or associates at a later date. Be assured, Hauptsturmführer Stangl, the pack will again form to reclaim its destiny. But for now you are a lone wolf."

"'...the bombs bursting in air...'" the girl on the radio sang, her voice very slightly trembling before once again steadying. It recalled for Stangl the fervent political rallies of the Reich's glory years—the rapturous upturned faces of boys in the Hitlerjugend, the rosy cheeks and soft thighs of their female counterparts in the Bund Deutscher Mädel. The uniform of an SS officer had impressed the girls. Stangl had enjoyed more than one of them, the memories of those intimate encounters recalling Gosia, whose cheeks were the rosiest, her thighs the softest. He'd forced Antoni to watch as his wife was taken the way a woman should be taken. The pathetic rodent had done nothing to stop it.

Typical Jew... Too spineless to protect their women, their children, or, indeed, themselves. We tried to do the world a favor. Can it not see?

This was a critical feature of National Socialist policy Stangl had tried to explain to the American journalist, Farley Sackstead, at a 1933 state dinner in Vienna. Radio would make Sackstead famous, but he was merely a newspaper correspondent then; indeed, the SS officer had been surprised to see him next to the Führer at the long dining table with Stangl at the journalist's opposite elbow. Later he learned that Hitler—Germany's new chancellor—had shrewdly orchestrated the seating assignment, angling for a featured interview in the prestigious *Chicago Tribune*. "It will increase my stature in the United States," the Führer told Stangl after the event. "Make Roosevelt think twice before crossing me."

Hitler had gotten his interview, Sackstead peppering the new chancellor with questions: *Why is Germany remilitarizing? Do you intend to abide by the Treaty of Versailles? Is Germany no longer a safe place for Jews?* Eventually the Führer had escaped to give his speech, giving Stangl an opportunity to engage the American in conversation. Many thought the handsome officer with his strong, unmistakably Aryan features and resplendent uniform to be the most impressive man in the SS corps, but Sackstead had seemed entirely indifferent. Furiously scribbling notes when speaking with Hitler, his reporter's pad and pencil had remained on the table as Stangl held forth.

"You American journalists do not understand National Socialism," the SS officer had proudly asserted. "You publish stories of beatings and violence, rare incidents entirely provoked by Communists and Jews. But you write nothing of our accomplishments here in Germany. Before National Socialism, this was a country without pride or purpose; indeed, we were near death. Now, we are rising from the ashes to again become proud Germans, pure of blood and spirit."

Stangl had tried to warn Sackstead of the danger Communists and Jews posed to both Germany and America, but the journalist dismissed the threat, with a terse comment, his voice edged.

"My wife is Jewish."

Afterward he'd put a space between them, giving Stangl his back in favor of a trivial conversation about art and cinema and books with one of Paul Goebbel's mistresses. "He's a traitor to his own race," Stangl told his wife later that night after returning to their apartment for a rare night in their shared bed.

From the radio in the guardroom, the voice of the singer echoed throughout the cellblock. She'd regained her footing after a slight hitch in her delivery, the tremor in her voice replaced by the same pride and passion Stangl felt when he and his fellow SS men launched into the stirring refrain of their marschiert. He began to sing.

"'Ha, ha, ha, ha, ha! Wir kämpfen für Deutschland, Wir kämpfen für Hitler.'" *Ha, ha, ha, ha, ha! We fight for Germany, We fight for Hitler.*

"Whatcha singin' there, Otto?"

Stangl looked to the eyes in the door slit. "That there yer national anthem?" the arschloch guard taunted, again in English. He began to sing along with the girl on the radio, his raw voice reverberating off the cinderblock walls of Stangl's cell.

"'...gave proof through the night....'"

Jimmy

Jenny's voice resounded through the airwaves, wondrously spanning the distance from Times Square to her brother's ears as he stood on the dark roadway outside Feucht Airfield. The magic of radio still fascinated Jimmy even though he'd never known a world without it. The idea of television was even more intriguing. Not long before she died Mom had taken Jimmy and his sister to an exhibit at the New York World's Fair, a bespectacled engineer inside the booth explaining how the new medium worked. "Television, or *TV* as we like to call it, employs the same basic principles as radio," he'd told them. "The camera is like a microphone, converting images, rather than audio, into radiowave signals. Like radio, the signals are then sent by a transmitter to a receiver, in this case a television."

Mom had been confused and nine-year-old Jenny uninterested, preening for the camera while casting sideways glances at her own black-and-white image on the television screen. But the explanation had made perfect sense to Jimmy, and after the canned presentation, he'd showered the engineer with so many questions the delighted technician eventually surrendered, his hands raised as if the thirteen-year-old hadn't been looking *for* answers so much as robbing him *of* them. "I see a future in this industry for a bright young kid like you," he'd told Jimmy before good-naturedly shooing the Doyles away so the next group could step before the eye of his experimental camera.

Listening to his sister's voice, Jimmy wondered if she faced a television camera in Times Square. Farley Sackstead was there, perhaps broadcasting for both radio and television. What would the TV audience think of the famous radio journalist? The deep, instantly recognizable voice evoked the image of a man like Orson Welles, someone large in both stature and personality. But when Sackstead showed up at the air base in Suffolk to interview Cap and the men of the *Daisy Mae*—a crew poised to break the record of forty-eight B-17 bomber missions—they'd been introduced to a somewhat small person with wire-rimmed glasses and thinning hair. "Seems more like a schoolteacher than a war correspondent," Cap had observed. The renowned journalist had asked a lot of questions that day, ending with one that provoked silence, the men of the *Daisy Mae* searching the floor of the barracks for answers.

"Do you ever stop being scared?"

After a few moments of what would later play as dead air on Sackstead's recording, Cap had responded.

"Nuthin' to be skeered of no more, Mister Sackstead. Them Krauts already threw what they had at us. They ain't got nuthin' left to throw."

After the journalist's return to London, the *Daisy Mae* had flown only one more bombing mission, a milk run sent to level an armaments works. Turned back before reaching their target when one of the plane's twelve-hundred-horsepower, nine-cylinder Wright engines began to sputter, the *Daisy Mae*'s official run of bombing sorties topped out at forty-six, three short of a new record.

"'…the bombs bursting in air,'" Jenny's voice rang out as Jimmy resumed walking, studying the night sky as he moved along the road. It was cloudless, the stars sparkling like diamonds on black velvet. In New York City he'd never seen a sky like this one, the tall metropolitan buildings offering mere wedges of the firmament, the coalesced aura of millions of city lights turning the stars into speckles of dust. *Good night for flying*, he mused, wondering where Project Casey Jones would send them in the morning. It promised to be a tough day regardless of destination. After celebrating the eve and early morning hours of V-E Day in nearby Nuremberg, the rest of the *Daisy Mae*'s crew would probably be half-drunk when they lifted off. Not Cap, of course. Jimmy knew their bomber pilot was already in his quarters, sleeping. The West Virginian didn't drink or carouse with the local girls, instead reading his Bible each night after writing a letter to his wife back in Morgantown. "The Lord don't look kindly on a boozehound, Jimmy," he'd told his youngest crew member more than once. "Besides, you boys all got parents. They'd never forgive me if I got y'all killed 'cause I was too drunk to fly right. Heck, I'd never forgive myself."

A sudden, sharp snap in the trees above the road startled him and Jimmy stopped, whirling around to face the sound. He lifted the flap of the holster on his belt and drew the .45 Cap had loaned him, his gun arm sweeping back and forth as if the weapon were a flashlight.

"Who's out there?" he called out, searching the darkness for the gleam of slitted eyes or the glint of moonlight on a telescopic sight.

An owl hooted.

"Show yourself!"

Jimmy had once claimed in a letter to his sister that he wasn't afraid inside his gun turret high above the earth with other B-17s around him in flames as they plummeted through the air, an occasional wing breaking loose and then spiraling lazily through the sky like a giant sycamore seed. *Our fate is decided one way or another,* he'd written Jenny. *Being scared won't protect us.* But he'd lied. Except for Cap, everyone on the *Daisy Mae* had been scared shitless on every bombing run from the time they entered enemy air space until they cleared it.

"'…gave proof through the night…'" his sister sang as Jimmy listened for the metallic sound of a Mauser's bolt action. He'd not forgotten the spine-stiffening fear that gripped him during those perilous seconds over a target, the sky peppered with exploding antiaircraft shells. He'd thought it behind him. But now, with the sanctuary of V-E Day still seconds away, he was once again scared shitless, peering into the black woods above the road while praying that the only predator lurking in the trees on this dimly moonlit night was the owl.

Gosia

"Now listen to me. Another contraction is starting," the midwife, Rita, said. She firmly cupped Gosia's chin, forcing the young woman to look at her. "Focus or I'll never get out of here."

Gosia shuddered free of the midwife's grip. Stangl had pinched her chin in the same way, forcing her to look at him as he'd writhed about atop her. He'd taunted her to the very last day of his tour at Sobibor.

"Du wirst mich vermissen, wenn ich weg bin, ja… Ich und mein großer schwanz?" *You will miss me when I'm gone, yes… Me and my big cock?*

His replacement, Obersturmführer Reichleitner, was a drunk but had run the camp with even greater precision than his predecessor. He'd immediately reassigned Antoni to the furniture shop but kept Gosia in his quarters as a maid, occasionally trying to have his way with her, a love affair with cognac dooming such encounters. The uprising was still more than a year away when he took over, but rumors of escape plans were common. Reichleitner dismissed them as flights of fancy and was lucky enough to be in Berlin when the revolt he'd disregarded finally happened. Nieman had been left in charge, the lascivious second-in-command immediately forcing Gosia into bed, where he discovered that she was menstruating. Disgusted, he banished her to the women's barracks where she was ostracized by the others as a collaborator. She was alone on a wooden sleeping platform when Antoni materialized from the shadows shortly after midnight on the 14th of October, 1943. He and Gosia had not seen each other in days and she was angry after learning that the uprising was to begin in less than sixteen hours. They'd briefly argued in whispers.

"Why was I not told?"

"I've not seen you, Gosia. How could I have—"

"Why didn't *someone* tell me...the women in these barracks. Why didn't they?"

"Most don't know. There may be informers among them. We've had to be careful."

"But *you* could have gotten word to me. You have ways. I know you do."

"Gosia, there's no time for this!"

Antoni had gone on, outlining the plan. It would begin in the late afternoon with officers targeted first, as many as possible killed without alerting the guards. Forged orders would then be presented at the gates that granted passage to a large work detail, ostensibly to labor for several days in the forest outside the camp. With no officers to dispute the orders, the guards were expected to comply and the first group of escapees would simply walk out of the camp with the guards watching. One of the organizers of the uprising, the Russian Soviet soldier, Pechersky, would lead the faux work detail.

"Stay with him, Gosia. Do not wait for me. Just go."

"I won't leave without you, Antoni."

"Gosia, please do what I say. I'll be at the rear of Lager I. It could be fifteen or twenty minutes before I reach the gates. You can't wait for me. Stay with Pechersky. He's promised to take care of you until I catch up. He believes the search will be concentrated to the west, so he and his men are going east… toward Ukraine. Go with them."

"No, I'll wait for you."

"Do not wait for me, Gosia. I will follow and catch up."

Gosia shuddered slightly as Rita rested a hand on her belly. "Get ready," the midwife said. Aunt Ewa translated and Gosia nodded. Pechersky had used the same words on the day of the uprising. "Get ready," he'd said as they were herded toward the camp gates by collaborating kapos. They were briefly delayed after the guards were given orders from Reichleitner's own typewriter, the SS officer's rabid scrawl duplicated on the signature line by an artist from Kraków. Then the gates were opened and they'd moved forward. "Don't look back," Pechersky murmured to her after they cleared the barricades. "If you hear shots, run. Otherwise, walk."

It had gone as planned until three trucks with canvas covers enclosing their rear beds approached the camp. Gosia was forty meters past the gates by then and moved to the side of the road along with the rest of the detail as panicky whispers bubbled up and spilled over.

"*Soldiers…*"

"*Quiet!*"

"*They know…*"

"*Shut up!*"

Suddenly shouts and then screams had sounded from inside the camp. Machine-gun fire followed and Pechersky had dashed ahead for the safety of the woods surrounding Sobibor.

"Forward for the Fatherland... Forward for Stalin!"

Gosia had chased after him along with the rest of the work detail, running frantically toward the forest with tracers whizzing past her ears and kicking up mud at her heels. Bullets hit bodies. Bodies hit the ground. The woman next to her fell, grabbing Gosia's wrist and pulling her down, a fountain of blood pulsing from a wound in her throat. Then Pechersky was there, shouting at Gosia in Russian as he jerked her free of the woman's grip, his words in Russian remembered for Antoni to later translate.

"Poshli, chert voz'mi!" *Let's go, goddammit!*

"'...gave proof through the night...'" the girl on the radio continued as the faint tingle of the next contraction began to surge. Gosia grasped the bedsheet handles.

"Poshli," she whispered to her unborn child, urging him to negotiate the last few centimeters through her pelvis and make good his escape. "Poshli, chert voz'mi!"

Zimmer

A web of drooping branches and darkness combined to provide cover for Zimmer as the singer's voice resounded from the distant loudspeakers at the airbase. After a few moments the American on the roadway resumed moving and Zimmer cautiously twisted his arm to reveal the watch face on the inside of his wrist. The iridescent hands were straight up.

Maybe it's over?

Hostilities against American, English, and French troops had stopped for the most part more than a week earlier, but he'd not reset the watch against another clock for days. And Russians in the east were still engaging, not just shooting at Germans but at anything that looked bad. If his watch were off by even a few seconds the American could legally murder him in these final, dwindling moments of the war. Zimmer smiled grimly. He and Braun had fought on two fronts for more than five years and been virtually unscathed. Now, on the last day of the conflict, the butcher's son from Berlin was likely dead, Zimmer perhaps about to join him. It would be funny, he thought, if grave markers weren't the punchline of the joke.

Unarmed and hidden in the woods, the irony of the hunter being hunted was not lost upon the young Wehrmacht soldier. In the fall of 1943, he, Braun, and Ilse Janning's brother, Karl, had been transferred from Trieste to scour the forest around Sobibor, helping to hunt down and capture escapees after the October uprising at the infamous death camp. The three infantrymen were initially happy with the new posting. At Trieste they'd battled partisans whose frustrating guerilla tactics produced high casualties among the German troops. However, Sobibor—until then an uncomfortable rumor for the three soldiers—turned the rumor into horrifying reality. The skeletal inmates and ominous odor hovering over Lager III prompted Zimmer's platoon to quietly agree among themselves that no escapees would be returned. "We'll bring back the ones that surrender on their own," their sergeant told them. "But nothing says we have to try very hard to find them."

It was a vow kept with merely a handful of fugitives taken into custody by Zimmer's squad, nearly all voluntarily surrendering. Still in ragged striped uniforms, the bedraggled men and women were exhausted and starving. Climbing down from trees, disinterring themselves from root cellars and outhouses, or emerging from barns with their hands up, they'd approached with eyes already dead. Filthy and emaciated, they were tired of running, tired of uncertainty, tired of life. Returned to the camp, they were immediately executed by the vengeful SS guards who had survived the uprising.

While most of the foot soldiers employed in the search were Wehrmacht troops like Zimmer, the officers in charge had all been SS. They were boastful and sadistic, and the regular army men had despised them. "They'd shit their pants in a battle where someone could shoot back," Braun observed after the first patrol. On one of the sorties Karl Janning—Ilse's brother—discovered a trembling man hiding in a haystack. He'd covered him with more hay, but the head of the entire operation—

SS Hauptsturmführer Franz Stangl—was with their group that day and saw it happen. "Drag that Jew cockroach out of there and bring him to me," he'd barked at Karl, afterward putting his Luger with its long silencer against the man's head and pulling the trigger. He'd then pointed the gun at Karl and shot him in the chest. "That's what happens to men who shirk their duty," he'd warned the surviving members of Zimmer's squad as Karl bled to death. Not long thereafter, Zimmer's entire platoon was sent to the eastern front. They didn't protest. "The weather will be brutal, but at least we'll shoot at someone who can fight back," Braun observed.

Zimmer studied the figure on the road below. He was likely a flyer, a good thing. Unlike infantrymen, the American Air Corps hadn't looked into their enemies' eyes or smelled their sweat. He might shoot at Zimmer, but it would be reactive—not the intentional act of a vengeful man but the impulsive response of a startled one.

So...don't startle him, idiot.

Zimmer cautiously lifted one leg, then eased it down, edging toward the shelter of a massive fir just a meter away. The duff on the forest floor was thick, his boot making a soft, crunching sound when he put his weight on it. He took another step, then froze when the sharp snap of a broken twig reverberated into the night. The American on the road below stopped and drew his sidearm, head swiveling until his gaze rested on the darkness that hid the young German. He called out, his words in English. An owl answered and the American called out again as the girl on the radio continued to sing, her voice cutting through the trees as if seeking Zimmer—indeed, as if she could illuminate his hiding place with song and give the shooter a clearer target. "'...gave proof through the night,'" she trilled and Zimmer held his breath, praying it was after midnight and the war was over, praying even harder that the American on the road knew it.

Riley

Riley had been in the city for two months when the Cat Woman left him the first note outside the rooftop shed where he slept in hot weather. Folded in half, she'd anchored it to the tarpapered surface with a brick fragment the color of dried blood. He'd tried to read it but couldn't, Mrs. Dworak later helping him with the bigger words.

> So this is a Laboratory!
> Why do you have to cut up helpless
> cats to find out how Human Beings work!
> I'm telling the Police!!!

He was in New York after washing out of boot camp, then washing out of Buffalo. At Fort Benning he'd marched, done push-ups, and actually fared well on the shooting range. But the weapon maintenance, even with Jimmy Doyle's help, was an unsolvable mystery, and with the drill sergeant constantly barking at him, Riley couldn't take apart his rifle and reassemble it without a mistake. Declared mentally unfit, he'd returned to Buffalo for a few months and worked the Lakes with Pap. Then Pap kicked him out too. Now he worked at Jakub Dworak's Kosher Delicatessen where he didn't have to take apart and reassemble the broom used to sweep the floor or the bucket of soapy water filled to wash windows.

The store was across the parking lot from CBS headquarters on East Fifty-Second Street. Once a shoe store run by the Cat Woman's father, the business space was on the ground level of a solidly built nineteenth-century edifice boasting stone arches on the main level and three floors of apartments above the street. Mr. Dworak had put a cot in the deli's storeroom for Riley, but there were no windows, and in warm weather the stockboy often slept on the building's flat roof or inside a large shed atop it, spaces between the wooden wall planks wide enough to allow a breeze to flow through. Often he rose in the middle of the night and sat on the parapet, legs dangling over the side as he surveyed the CBS parking lot below. A single house was on one corner of the lot, the only home left of the many that once graced the neighborhood. Both the building that housed the deli and the dilapidated residence belonged to the Cat Woman.

Her radio, tuned night and day to WCBS 880, had been airing a live soap opera when he replied to her inaugural message, securing it to the splintered porch of her house with a bottle. He'd checked the spelling with Mrs. Dworak. "Perfect, Riley," she'd told him. "Good job."

HELLO. I LIKE CATS. MY NAME IS RILEY BLAINE.

Afterward he'd returned to the roof of his building and watched as the Cat Woman's overcoat—dangling on a wire hanger from a flowerpot hook screwed into the low porch ceiling—gently swayed in an occasional breeze. It had been a sweltering summer, now two years past, the days hot and muggy, the rooftop at the mercy of the blistering sun. He'd perspired until his T-shirt was soaked but didn't seek shade, afraid to leave his post or look away lest she slip out the door, don her overcoat, and disappear. After several hours and with his bladder protesting, the Cat Woman's door opened enough for a broom handle to emerge, reaching out like the bony finger of a giant witch. It pushed the bottle over, then dragged the note across the unpainted planks of her porch until close enough for a veiny hand to reach out and snatch it up. The next morning, Riley found another note outside his shed, this one held in place by a small glass cat, its opalescent eyes peering at him as if the Cat Woman herself were inside the thing. It was his first note, ever, from a girl—albeit an old one—and even though it consisted of merely two words, it made him feel light and airy and full of possibility.

PROVE IT!

"'...the bombs bursting in air,'" Jenny sang on as Riley eyed the glass booth at the side of the stage. He was now close enough to see the Voice behind his desk, a microphone in front of him, its tubular shape reminiscent of vacuum cannisters the clerks at Macy's used to send messages from department to department. Riley loved Macy's, a place filled with sound and color and people who mostly ignored him as he wandered about, viewing the merchandise displays as if they were carnival exhibits. He liked the toy department best. It included a selection of cap pistols, and as he thought about them, Riley tightened his fingers around the handle of the gun in his pocket. *From here it shouldn't be hard,* he mused—not for a soldier who had qualified at the Fort Benning rifle range, hitting the bull's-eye ninety times out of one hundred. The Cat Woman's weapon was a handgun and not a rifle. Still, it shouldn't be hard.

He stole another look at Jenny over the suspended man's shoulder. "'...gave proof through the night,'" she sang as Riley edged toward a narrow crease separating the husky fellow from a blond woman next to him.

Not hard at all, he reassured himself. *Not from this close.*

Antoni

In the summer of 1943 the death camp at Belzec was closed with the last of its prisoners brought to Sobibor and executed. Shortly thereafter a note was found sewn into a coat sent to the sorting barracks. Its previous owner had been a kapo at Belzec.

We worked at Bełżec for one year and did not know where we would be sent next. They said it would be Germany. Now we are in Sobibor and know what to expect. Be aware that you will be killed also! Avenge us!

The Sobibor uprising had sprouted that day with the initial leaders envisioning a tunnel, a plan Pechersky, the Russian, quickly kiboshed. "It will take too long," he sniffed shortly after his arrival at the camp. "We'll all be in the gas chambers long before it's finished. Besides, escape through a tunnel will take too long. When it happens we'll have minutes, not hours. Like it or not, we must kill the guards and walk out." The majority of the conspirators, including Antoni Pietkowski, believed Pechersky was right, and the Red Army soldier—a Communist ideologue who could be strident and annoying—was put in charge. "He knows battle strategy and how to fight," Antoni later told Gosia.

The plan had evolved from there. The date was set, the uprising to begin an hour before evening roll call when as many SS officers as possible would be lured to separate locations in the camp, then killed with knives secured from the kitchen, axes from the forest details, hammers from the carpentry shop, and rifles smuggled out of the machine shop in a stovepipe. At roll call, the kapos would organize a sham work detail, ostensibly to encamp in the forest for several days. With no officers available, the conspirators believed the guards would not dispute the orders, allowing the detail to march unchallenged through the open gates with towermen watching from above. Meanwhile, those left behind would take the armory and use the weapons to kill the remaining guards. "There's no significant military complement nearby. Once we're out and all the guards are dead, everything changes. We'll have hours," Pechersky had speculated. "Maybe as much as a day.

It had started well. On the morning of the uprising Commandant Reichleitner was in Berlin, leaving Untersturmführer Nieman in charge. At dawn Antoni went to his job at the furniture shop in Lager I but left for the tailor shop around three p.m. He was waiting when Nieman, the hated second-in-command, rode up on a horse for the fitting of a leather coat he'd confiscated from a recent arrival.

"Waru mist er hier?" Nieman had asked when he saw Antoni. *Why is he here?*

"To repair a table," the tailor answered in German. He'd then asked Niemen to remove his gun belt in order to properly fit the jacket. Nieman did and Antoni moved quickly, burying an axe in the SS officer's head. Afterward he and the tailor made for the gates, only to discover that the plan had fallen apart.

"'...the bombs bursting in air,'" the girl on the radio sang as Antoni listened from the bench just outside the cellblock. Bombs had burst on the day of the uprising too. About half the ersatz work detail had cleared the gates when a trio of German army supply trucks rumbled down the road leading to the camp. Prisoners still inside the fences panicked, believing the trucks were filled with reinforcements sent to kill them. They rushed the gates, and when the tower guards opened fire with their machine guns, hundreds made for the fences, knocking them down and then racing into the minefields surrounding the facility. Dozens were blown apart, dozens more shot as they made for the woods one hundred meters to the east. What had been carefully planned disintegrated into chaos. Of the 600 inmates, only 300 escaped. Antoni was among them after retrieving one of the smuggled rifles from a fallen comrade, shooting a watchtower guard, and then killing another by smashing his skull with the gunstock. Afterward he'd tossed the rifle aside and then dashed through a minefield littered with bodies and body parts.

"'…gave proof through the night,'" the American girl on the radio sang, the military policeman on duty singing along with her. Suddenly Stangl's voice thrust a competing anthem into the air, his percussive delivery identifying it as something military.

"Wonder if he'll be singing that tune when they put a noose around his neck?" the major remarked from the doorway. Antoni looked at the American officer as if he'd not understood the words.

"What's wrong, Antoni?"

Antoni didn't answer, instead trying to shut out Stangl's rabid growl by visualizing Gosia and the child they would share—indeed, who might already have been born. Instead, he was suddenly running once again through a field of mutilated corpses, stumbling over bodies, his ears filled with the buzz of bullets that missed and the dull thuds of those that didn't—the safety of the forest so close and yet so out of reach as Stangl proudly bellowed the anthem of the Third Reich's black-uniformed Schutzstaffel.

"'Ha, ha, ha, ha, ha! Wir kämpfen für Deutschland, Wir kämpfen für Hitler.'"

"Antoni?" the major repeated. "Antoni?"

4

7 May 1945

1759:31 to 1759:40 Eastern Standard Time
2359:31 to 2359:40 Central European Time

Farley

"'...that our flag was still there,'" young Jenny Doyle sang as Farley recalled meeting her brother, Jimmy. He'd traveled to High Wycombe Air Base in England for a series of radio interviews with a B-17 crew on the verge of breaking the record for most missions in a Flying Fortress. The kid had impressed him. He'd graduated early from high school, then delayed college in favor of enlistment. Nineteen years old at the time of the interview, he planned to pursue a college degree after the war. Intrigued by a television exhibited at the New York World's Fair in 1939, the young airman foresaw a career in the new medium. "I predict television will replace radio for the most part," he'd contended. "Especially for your profession. You know...news and public service stuff."

"Are you interested in broadcast journalism?" Farley had asked, keeping secret Bill Paley's proposal of a televised news program hosted by the wartime voice of CBS Radio in Europe. The kid wasn't.

"No, I'd prefer the engineering side of things... Figuring out how to make the screens bigger, the pictures clearer."

Farley watched the girl on the stage. He'd seen her name in his script notes and wondered if she and Jimmy were related, his first glimpse of the young woman confirming the shared bloodline. The sister and brother had the same reddish hair, blue eyes, and angular Irish features: pointed chins, long noses.

Farley's serendipitous link to both siblings wasn't surprising. Everywhere he'd gone during the war—North Africa, the beach at Anzio not long after the invasion, Normandy less than two weeks after D-Day, a liberated Paris—he'd stumbled upon people connected to a story he'd already covered.

He'd interviewed Antoni and Gosia Pietkowski as part of a report on the harrowing uprising at Sobibor only to be reminded of a 1933 dinner in Berlin where the newsman had been seated between a tall, movie-star handsome SS officer and the newly installed chancellor of Germany, Adolph Hitler. The dinner—a banquet-style event to celebrate Hitler's recent inauguration—had given Farley an opportunity to interview the Nazi leader, the burgeoning Führer providing stilted responses to the reporter's questions while slurping from his water goblet and chewing with his mouth open, food spilling onto his brown uniform blouse with its party medallion and swastika armband. "Until he gets behind a podium with a microphone, he's as unimpressive a man as I've ever encountered," Farley later told his wife. "Afterward he's the most terrifying."

Hitler didn't return to his seat after his speech and Farley was subsequently subjected to a barrage of virulent opinions from the SS officer at his opposite elbow. Eventually he managed to extricate himself, moving to Hitler's empty chair where he was immediately ensnared in another web, spun by a chatty aide to Hitler's propaganda chief, Paul Goebbels. A beautiful woman, she'd demonstrated a rapacious eagerness to sleep with the *Chicago Tribune*'s foreign correspondent if he could get her out of Germany. Farley had wriggled free of her net by flashing his wedding ring, afterward beating a hasty path to the exit. He'd forgotten about the SS officer, Franz Stangl, until the man's name was disinterred during the meeting with Antoni and Gosia.

The interview with the Polish couple had taken place in Yorkshire where they were housed with a host family after British intelligence spirited them out of Europe, hoping to recruit Antoni and his translator's skills to MI-6 before the American

OSS could latch on to him. The former interpreter at Sobibor was perhaps the most purposeful man Farley had ever met, never breaking eye contact, his thick eyebrows forming a single hedgerow when he furrowed his forehead in thought. Antoni had impassively recounted the terrifying day when soldiers dragged them from their apartment, their years in the Warsaw ghetto, the packed cattle train transport to Sobibor, and their first exposure to the man they came to know as the White Death: Franz Stangl.

Gosia had clung to Antoni during the interview. The young woman spoke little to no English, Farley's questions and her almost whispered responses translated by her husband. When Stangl's name came up she'd stood and left the room, later returning with the couple's Yorkshire hosts, a chatty pair anxious to make their own debuts on network radio. Farley had obliged them, pretending to listen, his eyes flickering back and forth between the two nattering hosts and Gosia. *She is very beautiful,* he later wrote Marta, *but even though her face has no marks, she seems scarred.* After returning to London, he'd edited the Yorkshire couple from the on-air broadcast, recalling the final thought Antoni shared with him.

"There are Stangls everywhere…in Poland, in Germany and Russia, even here in this little village."

Outside the broadcast booth the dark-eyed boy just behind the front row of spectators on the street continued to steal glances at the singer on the stage, peeking over the shoulder and then ducking behind the large man with an oval name patch over the pocket of his shirt. The night was warm, but the boy wore an oversized winter coat, its lower edge well below his knees. His face was beaded with sweat. "'Oh say does that…'" Jimmy Doyle's little sister continued as the second hand on the huge clock at the rear of the stage met the *8* on its dial with the dark-eyed boy bobbing up and down, his movements so in cadence with the rhythm of the young woman's song it seemed he might be dancing with her. Twenty seconds were left until midnight in Europe and the end of the war.

Selma

The sound of exploding firecrackers made it seem as if bombs were actually bursting in the air of Manhattan. Selma put the Roger down and resumed her watch from the living room picture window. Earlier, Fifty-Second Street had been crowded, but as six p.m. approached millions of New Yorkers were huddled by their radios, thousands more in Times Square, all of them listening to fifteen-year-old Jenny Doyle sing "The Star-Spangled Banner." Only one car was left in the CBS lot as Selma peeked between the curtains, puzzled by flashes of memory. Tidy homes had once been there, all in a row. Friends had lived in some of them, their names lost in a fog that thickened by the day.

Millie? Audrey... or Angela?

Her friends' parents had long ago taken the money from real estate developers and left, their neat little homes razed to make room for progress. Selma's father had been offered money too. But he'd refused to sell the house where Selma and her brother were born, a decision less representative of sentiment than obstinance, a temperament more appealing than currency to an inherently obstinate man.

Years later, long after unwed and pregnant Selma had been banished to a Lower East Side tenement apartment with Carl, her parents both succumbed to the Spanish flu, the house and building passing through probate and then to the sole survivors: Selma and her brother. Notified by the lawyer, Owen returned to New York after more than twenty years away, accompanied by his son. Her nephew would be in his forties now, Selma calculated, but the wispy, fair-haired boy was not yet eighteen back then. He'd had an unexpectedly deep voice, excellent manners, and eyes that seemed to catalogue all they surveyed. *It isn't fair,* Selma still brooded, her brother given a child while her only chance to be a mother had been stolen.

Selma's brother had stayed in New York for two weeks to

help her sort out their parents' affairs. Overruling Carl, who wanted to sell the house and apartment building, Owen had generously signed over his share of the properties to his sister. "Carl's an idiot," he told his sister. "Don't sell. The rents will support you for the rest of your life." After her brother left, Selma never again saw him, although for years he sent letters on her birthday and at Christmas. The correspondences abruptly ended in late 1938, an obituary along with a short note from Owen's widow arriving in early 1939. A few more years passed before she heard more from his son, the boy with the deep voice and penetrating eyes.

"'...that our flag was still there,'" the girl on the radio sang as Selma studied the apartment building she'd inherited. The window of the second-floor apartment where the young Polish woman labored was still open, and as Selma watched, the Jew's wife leaned out and took in a few large gulps of air. She wondered if a radio played in the room. A child would be born on this night, perhaps with the Voice in its ear. It was a disturbing notion that resurrected the words of Reverend Dodge.

"The little child is the most vulnerable, the most in need of the Miracle Holy Water. Sprinkle it on their innocent heads. Dab it onto their sweet lips."

Selma reached into the pocket of her housecoat, a flock of cats instantly surrounding her, awaiting a treat. Meowing plaintively, they stood on their hind legs and pawed at her, their claws penetrating her leggings and the parchment-like skin beneath it. When Selma's hand emerged holding a vial of Miracle Holy Water rather than food, the meows crescendoed into yowling, and she uncapped the vial and shook it, a tiny rainstorm cascading downward. Most of it landed on a big tom who arched his back and hissed in protest, his teeth bared.

"Don't you sass me, Sidney!" Selma snapped. "Don't you dare sass me!"

The Sidney retreated and Selma went to the kitchen, retrieving three more vials of Miracle Holy Water from a cigar box on the counter. Afterward she cut a path to the front door through the swarm of cats, gently sweeping them out of the way with a foot.

"The little child is the most vulnerable…"

On the front porch Selma's long overcoat hung on its hanger. She took it down and pulled it on.

"Sprinkle it on their innocent heads. Dab it onto their sweet lips."

With the vials of Miracle Holy Water in one of the overcoat's wide pockets, Selma headed for the apartment building on the other side of the parking lot, the voice of the young singer in Times Square trailing her out the open door of her rundown home and then merging with output from the loudspeakers mounted on the outside of the CBS building, an almost imperceptible hitch in the girl's delivery as the top of the hour approached.

"'Oh, say does that…'"

JENNY

Jenny watched her father as she sang. Tears streaked his cheeks, his nose turning red as the Irishman cried. Always an emotional man, quick to laugh or cry, his tears had come more often in the last few months and Jenny knew there wasn't much time left. She loved her outgoing father, had loved him even in the days when he was off the wagon. Never a mean drunk, Brian Doyle was easy to love. But Jenny had never counted on him until Jimmy left for the army. She wouldn't be able to count on him much longer. She knew his liver would soon betray him no matter how hard he tried to make up for lost time.

Jenny had accepted that her father's death would be unlike her mother's. With Dad, Jenny would grieve, knowing it would pass. But the loss of her mother remained with her, a living, aching thing deep inside. "Cardiomyopathy," the doctor had explained to the Doyles after all the tests were completed and the cause of Siobhan Doyle's fatigue and shortness of breath were identified. He'd tossed out the word as if absolving himself, as if naming the hangman somehow lessened the impact of the hanging. "Nothing much we can do," he'd added, afterward prescribing medicines that were inexorably less effective as Siobhan Doyle's heart weakened. Eventually Jenny's mother sensed an imminence her family refused to accept and sat her children down for the talk they'd both dreaded. Jenny had been eleven years old, Jimmy fifteen. "You must not wallow in self-pity for long," she'd advised. "Your father will wallow long enough for the two of you."

She'd seemed prescient, her husband responding to her death with fading interest in his job and mounting interest in whiskey. Eventually laid off, the family was forced to subsist for a time on Siobhan's modest life insurance benefit and Jimmy's two part-time jobs. But the war changed things. Even before Jimmy's deployment, Brian Doyle put aside his bottle and got his union job back—showing up on time, bringing his paycheck home for Jenny to deposit, and providing a strong shoulder for his daughter to lean on when Jimmy's train pulled out of Penn Station on its way to Fort Benning, Georgia. Now the war in Europe—Jimmy's war—was over. *They're keeping the Daisy Mae at a base here in Germany*, he'd recently written. *We'll be part of a special operation.* The rest of the letter had been redacted, save his closing.

Jenny let her eyes drift down to the array of microphones sending her voice across the globe. The logo of the fledgling ABC network was among them along with its more venerable competitors, NBC and CBS. Jenny was excited that the famous CBS newsman, Farley Sackstead, was covering the V-E celebration in Times Square. She'd earlier seen him climb the steps to the stage and go into the glass-walled radio booth. The famous broadcaster had surprised her, looking nothing like his radio voice. She'd expected someone tall and movie star handsome like Walter Pidgeon, one of the stars of the wartime hit *Mrs. Miniver*. However, Sackstead's thinning hair, wire-rimmed glasses, and slight build were more reminiscent of Walter Brennan than Walter Pidgeon. He'd waved and smiled when he saw her standing next to a production assistant in the opposite wing, and despite the absence of matinee idol looks, Jenny had been thrilled.

"That's Farley Sackstead," she'd gushed to the PA, a young woman not much older than Jenny, a series of lit cigarettes she never puffed scissored between the fingers of one hand. A walking compendium of bored sighs and eye-rolling, her name was Claudia.

"Yeah...no kidding," Claudia replied.

"My brother met him...in England. Mister Sackstead interviewed Jimmy and his entire crew. That's my brother...Jimmy."

"That's great, honey. Listen...you won't forget the lyrics, right? People always forget the lyrics when they see the crowd. So you know them, right? You've got them nailed down?"

"I know them."

"'Cause people always panic and forget when they get in front of an audience."

"I won't panic."

"People do."

"I sang before a full house at Yankee Stadium," Jenny huffed. "I finished the entire song in one minute and twenty-two seconds. I didn't forget anything."

The PA shrugged. "Don't blow a fuse, honey. I'm just trying to help."

"'...that our flag was still there,'" Jenny sang to the thousands assembled. She was grateful for the cotton wadded into her ears, something Mrs. Petroff had suggested. There were two huge amplified speakers on the stage with smaller ones mounted on streetlights and buildings. Their combined output produced an echo that reverberated around the square and then back at her. "The voice in your head will be a fraction of a second in front of the one coming from the speakers," Mrs. Petroff had warned her star student. "Don't get confused. Keep your focus *inside* your head, not outside it." Despite the cotton, it was not easy and Jenny felt herself losing focus. She concentrated harder, separating the voice in her head from the disembodied one coming from the speakers—so intent on her task, she didn't stumble when the dark eyes and thatch of sooty black hair once again popped up over her father's shoulder.

STANGL

Stangl lay down on his side in the narrow bunk and covered his head with the thin pillow to dampen the voice of the girl on the radio. It made things worse. The bunk's metal frame was bolted to the cement floor, and vibrations prompted by sound waves were transmitted up the legs and into his skull until it seemed as if the singer were inside his brain. Some words in German and English were similar and he'd understood one of the lyrics. The American "flag was still there." Stangl grimaced as if in pain. All over Europe the distinctive flag of the Third Reich was being torn down and replaced by the American Stars and Stripes, the British Union Jack, the French Tricolore, and the hated Russian Hammer-and-Sickle. Under the blood-red Nazi banner, with its unapologetic black swastika on a white disc of purity, the proud German forces had marched into Europe's capitals, their jackboots slamming against cobblestoned streets in rhythmic precision, the sound echoing across a conquered and cowering populace. In most cases, little to no resistance was mounted and Stangl had once asked Antoni to explain. "There was no reason to resist, Herr Hauptsturmführer," Antoni had offered. "The German troops were obviously invincible."

Antoni's tone had been measured, his subservience bordering on sarcasm, and Stangl had unholstered his sidearm and struck him on the head, knocking him to the floor.

"Lüg mich nicht an du, Judenschwein!" *Don't lie to me, Jew pig!*

With blood dripping down his forehead Antoni had slowly regained his feet that day, leveling stony eyes at the commandant.

"We are patient people, Hauptsturmführer. Tomorrow is coming."

Stangl had nearly killed him for such insolence, placing the barrel of his Luger against the Jewish translator's skull, his finger on the trigger.

"Sich entschuldigen, Judenschwein!" he'd barked. *Apologize, Jew pig!*

Antoni had refused to apologize and his defiant silence curiously saved him, surprising Stangl enough to give him pause, the interlude helping the commandant realize that Gosia's grief might become so tiresome he'd have to kill her too. "I see no tomorrows for you people in this place, Antoni," he'd taunted as he re-holstered his pistol. "You shamble to your deaths like sheep on their way to the disinfectant chutes."

After receiving news of the uprising at Sobibor, Stangl had regretted letting Antoni live, worried his translator would find him along with the tomorrow he'd promised. The former commandant had been gone for over a year at the time of the mass escape, but culpability for the revolt cast a wide net and he'd been summoned to Berlin along with Reichleitner to face SS Chief Heinrich Himmler. Both escaped a firing squad. Reichleitner was transferred to Italy where a partisan's bullet to the head carried out the sentence he deserved while Stangl was ordered to supervise the capture and disposal of escapees. "Clean up your mess!" the fearsome head of the Schutzstaffel had added, an accusation that still rankled.

It was not my mess, Reichsführer Four-Eyes! You put Reichleitner in charge! What did you expect?

Upon his return to Sobibor, Stangl had organized a search that was quickly threatened by insubordination, the soldiers assigned to the duty, other than officers, all drawn from the Wehrmacht. Unenthusiastic about their mission, they preferred to overlook rather than overtake, necessitating Stangl's direct involvement. After assuming command of a search party, he'd shot one of the mutinous soldiers when the man allowed a fugitive to remain hidden in a mound of loose hay. Following the incident his aide recommended he keep to his quarters. "No point risking friendly fire," he'd cautioned.

The operation had been a moderate success, all but fifty-eight of the insurgents killed on sight or returned to captivity for immediate execution. Gosia's name hadn't appeared on the roster of those recaptured or killed and Stangl had been relieved; indeed, in the nineteen months since, he had spent many hours contriving fantasies in which they were reunited—impure and dangerous thoughts that too often invaded his slumber. Stangl knew he talked in his sleep and while still on active duty had worried he'd unconsciously confess his love for her, subsequently awakening to a firing squad. Sleeping pills eventually banished Gosia from his dreams, but daytime fancies persisted, veering into the wistful. Too often he imagined a world in which she was not a Jew…or one in which Franz Stangl was not a man morally bound to exterminate her.

Stangl heard the American major's voice coming from the direction of the guardroom outside the cellblock. He uncovered his head and rolled over. The arschloch guard's eyes were no longer in the view slit of his cell door.

"'Oh, say does that Star-Spangled…'"

He sat up and forced the blasphemous thoughts of Gosia Pietkowski from his head, replacing them with the proud words of a different hymn. He was not a Jew lover. He was a loyal soldier, a good German who had faithfully followed orders and done his duty. It was not his fault. She was a witch—a Jewess who'd cast a spell over him.

"'Ha, ha, ha, ha, ha! Wir kämpfen für Deutschland,'" he whispered, mining the lyrics of the SS Marschiert for courage and triumph. "'Ha, ha, ha, ha, ha! Wir kämpfen für Hitler,'" he continued, unearthing only despair.

Jimmy

"Show yourself!" Jimmy called out again. "Show yourself or I'll shoot!" There was no answer, not even from the owl. The road had a wide, flat shoulder covered in high grass and weeds, then a knee-high embankment to reach a slope that angled gently upward to the forest. Jimmy dashed for the shoulder and flung himself into the grass. Pressing his body against the ground as if the damp earth could absorb him, he listened for the snap of another twig or the soft brush of footsteps cautiously moving over the thick forest duff. He heard only Jenny's voice, coming from the distant loudspeakers. She was nearing the end of the national anthem.

"'...that our flag was still there.'"

He could run for it. The air base was an eighth of a mile off, a scant two hundred twenty yards, the sharp curve—partially illuminated by the gate spotlights—perhaps fifty yards away. A sprinter in high school, Jimmy Doyle had placed third in the New York City scholastic track meet of 1942. He'd run the 220 in 22.3 seconds. It was a John Adams High School record, and afterward, the track coach at Fordham approached. "Keep working, son, and there might be a scholarship for you in a couple of years," he'd said, offering a few training tips and then suggesting that the young sprinter's big feet predicted more height and leg length. "Longer distances might be in your future. Heck, I wager you'll be a formidable 440 or even 880 man down the road." It didn't happen. Jimmy didn't get taller, his big feet not harbingers of the future but inheritances from his father. College didn't happen either. He graduated from John Adams at seventeen and then enlisted. Less than a year later his five feet eight inches and big feet were in the belly turret of a B-17 bomber.

Jimmy cautiously lifted his head and searched the darkness, Cap's .45 in his hand. The moon was a slender scimitar, its pale light offering little help. In basic training they'd drilled on nights like this one, their sergeant ordering them to disassemble their weapons and then reassemble them in the dark. "Be ready to do this blindfolded," he'd insisted. "The goddamned Krauts ain't gonna hold a flashlight for y'all." Poor Riley Blaine hadn't been able to do it and the sergeant—a foul-tempered Southerner who hated Yankees—laid into the shy Buffalo, New York native after the platoon's first night-time drill. During a storm the next night he'd awakened everyone in the barracks at three a.m. and hustled them outdoors where they took apart their weapons and put them back together over and over. Despite Jimmy's help, Riley couldn't get it right. The following night the sergeant again ordered the recruits from their bunks and onto the parade ground. "Y'all can send Private Blaine a thank-you card," he told them. "Sooner he gets it right, the sooner you fellers can get back to dream-fuckin' yer girlfriends." After four sleepless nights in a row a few of the boys went after Riley, blackening his eyes and loosening a tooth before Jimmy and a couple of others pulled them off. The next day the hapless draftee was kicked out—sent home with his army fatigues, a train ticket to Buffalo with a layover in New York, and a dishonorable discharge branding him as mentally unfit.

"When you reach New York you can stay overnight with my family," Jimmy offered before Riley left. "I'll have my sister meet you at the station. It'll be better than spending the night on a bench in the depot." Afterward he phoned Jenny to let her know she'd been volunteered. "Meet him at the station, then get him back there in the morning, sis. Don't just write instructions. He's not much of a reader, you know? He's…slow."

"You mean retarded?"

"Don't use that word, Jenny. It may not seem like it at first… Riley won't show it…but he's pretty sensitive. Sarge gave him hell while he was here. I suspect people have been giving him hell all his life. So be nice. Let him stay the night, then put him back on the train."

Still prone, Jimmy lifted his head and shoulders enough to see over the top of the high grass and weeds. There was movement in the forest above the road and he ducked back down, praying he'd seen a branch swaying in a breath of wind, an owl feathering its wings, or a restless squirrel. Even a bear or a wolf—any creature other than the most dangerous of them all: man.

"'Oh, say does that…'"

Jimmy felt his heart quicken, pounding so loudly in his ears he wondered if the man in the woods could hear it too. It *was* a person, he was now convinced—not a branch or an owl or a squirrel—but a German soldier.

Surrendering? Trying to get home?

There was no reason for them to shoot at each other. Mere seconds remained until zero hundred hours and the official cessation of hostilities. Nevertheless, the young airman carefully cocked the hammer of Cap's .45, wincing when the mechanical click reverberated into the night.

We've no reason to shoot each other…no reason at all, he rationalized, hoping the German felt the same way.

Gosia

"'…that our flag was still there,'" the girl on the radio sang. Gosia wondered if a flag now flew over the former death camp at Sobibor. A blood-red Nazi flag with its prominent swastika had prosecuted the sky on the day of the uprising, rippling vaingloriously in a light breeze as three hundred Jews escaped. Walking and then running after the gunfire began, Gosia had reached the woods to find Pechersky waiting despite protests from his fellow Soviet soldiers. "Leave her. She'll just slow us down," one grumbled, and at first Pechersky had refused, keeping a promise made to Antoni to look after her. But once they set out Gosia couldn't keep up, staggering over the uneven forest floor and fallen trees in a striped camp dress and thin-soled slippers, the bramble bushes scratching her arms, the thorny vines tearing at her ankles. Several times she'd fallen and eventually the frustrated Russians huddled together, complaining to Pechersky in whispers until he broke free and approached her. "Wait here. I'll find shelter and come back," he'd instructed, pressing a knife fashioned from metal roofing and wood strips into her hand.

He never returned, and with nightfall Gosia had set off on her own, searching for the north star. "Keep it on your left," Antoni had taught her. "That will put you on a course to Ukraine." Gosia had tried. But the forest canopy was too dense, the unreadable stars splattered across slivers of sky between the branches. Eventually she'd given up and taken shelter in the hollow of a massive tree that blocked the moon and cast her into darkness. With first light still three hours off, she'd remained awake and motionless for a time, listening for howling dogs or the crunch of jackboots on the forest floor. Then sleep overtook her, her slumber dreamless. She'd awakened in the gray of dawn, the forest silent save the twitter of birds. Despairing, she accepted that Pechersky had abandoned her and that Antoni was dead. Then she'd remembered her husband's promises.

The Americans will be here today, Gosia.

"Muszę spróbować," she'd murmured to the silent trees as she disentangled herself from the hollow of the tree and stood.

The Americans will be here tomorrow.

"Muszę spróbować." *I must try.*

It had been as much prayer as self-rebuke, and as if God were listening Gosia had inexplicably and wondrously been answered.

"I'm here, Gosia… I'm here. There's a farm nearby. They will hide us. I'm here."

Antoni had not come alone that morning, bringing along Janusz—a stout, red-cheeked man in overalls. He'd not been happy to be there, growling at them as he warily searched the forest.

"Stop talking…sound carries in these woods."

Afterward Janusz had set out, expertly avoiding each downed tree, gnarled root, and twisting vine as he glided through the early-morning forest like a blind man negotiating his own living room. Gosia and Antoni had both struggled to keep up, Gosia convinced that the big farmer was trying to lose them in the woods. Antoni reassured her.

"He won't leave us. Tillie…his wife…she wouldn't like it."

Less than an hour later they'd reached the farm where Gosia met Tillie and realized that she'd been right. Given a choice, Janusz would have left them in the forest. But Antoni had been right too. Tillie—a broad-faced woman as cheery as Janusz was curt—would have been furious with her husband had he done it.

Gosia looked at the clock atop the dresser. It was almost six o'clock—midnight in Europe where Antoni now worked for the American army. Above the dresser was one of Aunt Ewa's paintings. It depicted a slender, spectral figure alone in a flat wasteland, a sober offering from a normally sunny person. In Poland before the war, Aunt Ewa and Uncle Jakub had lived in the same house as Gosia and her family, and in some ways the little woman had been more a mother to her than her actual mother, imbuing her niece with feistiness and a passion for art and music. Gosia both loved and admired her aunt, and after a few days on the farm she grew to love and admire Tillie too. The farmer's wife was efficient and tireless. Within twenty-four hours she'd altered clothes from her closet and Janusz's to fit Gosia and Antoni, assigned the fugitive couple chores to perform, and put a plan in place to explain their presence on the farm.

"If neighbors ask, you're our cousins from Krakow. If the Germans come, you hide in the silo."

Gosia envied Tillie and her aunt. Between them the two women had given birth to seven children without the help of doctors or hospitals, while Gosia couldn't persuade one stubborn baby to trade his present accommodation for a roomier one. "Muszę spróbować," she muttered as the tension in the walls of her womb began to spread. She gripped the bedsheets, praying for Antoni to once again miraculously appear and lead their child to safety. Meanwhile, the girl on the radio sang on, celebrating an America unaware of the new citizen ready to claim its birthright if the immigrant, Gosia Pietkowski, could push a bit harder for just a bit longer.

"Get ready," Rita, the midwife, said.

Gosia understood her words without translation and prepared herself, waiting for her contraction to build, at the same time wondering where the father of her child might be as six p.m. in New York City and midnight across the Atlantic approached.

ZIMMER

The American called out again, then abandoned the moonlight and dashed to the edge of the road, taking cover in the high grass and weeds on the shoulder. Once again Zimmer prayed, this time beseeching the Almighty to restrain the enemy soldier from randomly spraying the dark forest with bullets. The veteran German infantryman had seen more than one man killed by an unaimed bullet, had perhaps killed one himself after a Russian sniper in a church belltower pinned down his squad in Belarus. After the marksman picked off every man, save Zimmer and Braun, the two Wehrmacht soldiers held their Mausers over their heads, firing blindly until a bullet miraculously killed the sniper. It was dumb luck, but word of the incident filtered up to high command, and with Berlin desperate for good news to feed the German public, the infantrymen were recommended for decoration. A pair of Honor Clasps, along with a reporter and a photographer, were sent to the front where they found no tunics on which to pin the medals. Both men had deserted.

A day earlier Braun had roused Zimmer just before dawn, kneeling beside him in a shallow bunker scraped from clay-hard ground, his Mauser leaning against the earthen wall of their foxhole. "Leave yours too," he'd advised. Zimmer had taken his weapon, even though he had no ammo. "I'd feel naked without it," he'd justified to his friend, but it was short-lived devotion. Zimmer had shrapnel acquired in Belgium lodged in one hip, and his weapon weighed more than four kilograms. The combination joined to an uneven forest floor rendered his gait lopsided, and when his slight limp became more pronounced, Braun grew impatient.

"Get rid of that goddamned thing! You're slowing us down!"

And Zimmer had, tossing the rifle into the underbrush and then putting it out of his mind as if it were just another fallen comrade.

The girl's voice coming from the distant loudspeakers now seemed otherworldly, a siren on the rocks rather than a songstress singing into a microphone.

"'...that our flag was still there.'"

The young Wehrmacht soldier breathed quietly through an open mouth, soft rushes inaudible from more than a few inches away as he cautiously took another step toward the broad trunk of the nearby fir tree. He paused to search for movement in the roadside grass, at the same time rehearsing the English words Braun had taught him before they deserted.

I give up.

His heart racing, he took another step.

I give up…Ich gebe auf…I give up.

He doubted his father would approve of surrender. A veteran of the first war, the elder Zimmer's voice rang with pride when he spoke of his military service. "We charged into No Man's Land, proud to die if necessary for the Kaiser," he'd claimed. The old man had been an ardent supporter of Hitler from the beginning, proud the Führer no longer felt it necessary to wallow in World War I shame imposed by vengeful England and France, prouder still that his country's chancellor believed in Germany's manifest destiny and the proud traditions of the German army. After the Night of Broken Glass he'd been more circumspect but still a believer, closing the window shutters so he wouldn't have to watch as Jewish friends and neighbors were taken away in trucks, the disturbing stories of gas chambers and ovens shrugged off. "Communist lies!" he'd insisted.

Zimmer had last seen his father on a short leave between the mop-up duty at Sobibor and his transfer to the eastern front. During the visit he'd described the camp at Sobibor and the assassination of Karl Janning by the SS officer they called the White Death. He'd hoped to relax the Führer's grip on the old man. Instead, Wilhelm Zimmer grew progressively uneasy, eyes shifting back and forth between the Bible in his lap and a window that opened onto the street. "What can one do?" he'd lamented. "The Führer must have a good reason for such places to exist." When his son continued to argue, the elder Zimmer had put a finger to his lips, lowering his voice to a whisper. "Be careful with your opinions. People are watching. They are listening."

Zimmer glanced at the radiant hands of his watch. The big hand had nudged past the *12*.

The war must be over…unless my watch is fast.

"'Oh, say does that…'" the American girl singer continued as Zimmer remained fixed in place and silent, searching the high grass on the roadside for signs of movement.

I give up… I give up. Ich gebe auf… I give up.

Suddenly a click echoed across the space that separated him from the American. Zimmer stiffened. The sound—the hammer of a pistol being cocked—was unmistakable.

I give up… I give up. Ich gebe auf… I give up.

Riley

The exchange of notes with the Cat Woman had been followed by an invitation to her house. Now Riley spent most evenings with her. They listened to the radio, wandered the streets of Manhattan after midnight, sometimes went to movies. She'd told him about the Voice. He'd told her about the army and Jenny. She was his best friend.

He'd first heard about her plan to kill the Voice in the fall, summoned to her house by another note left outside the rooftop shed.

Come over tonight

After work he'd crossed the CBS parking lot and shuffled up the slumping steps that clung precariously to the Cat Woman's porch. The place, then and now, had been in an advanced state of disrepair. Flaps of window screens hung loose, nail heads were extruded from warped planks on the porch, and the front door sagged so severely Riley could see the interior of the house through an open space beneath the header. He'd knocked and heard a chorus of meowing cats inside the home, then the Cat Woman opened the door. Cradling a tawny tom who looked at Riley as if he hated him, she, too, had been in an advanced state of disrepair—her slightly hooked nose and long tangle of gray hair rendering her more witch than woman. She'd held out the tom, putting the cat's face next to Riley's.

"Can't get over it."

"Over what?"

"Never mind… Come inside."

He'd followed her into a living room where balls of cat fur gathered under the coffee table, lurked in corners, and dangled like hirsute Christmas ornaments from the blades of an idle ceiling fan. "Wait here," she'd ordered, afterward going upstairs while Riley sat on her lumpy sofa and stared at the charred carcass of a Barcalounger next to a table topped by two books. Her cathedral-shaped radio had been on, honey-voiced men singing about a paper doll with flirty eyes. When the Cat Woman returned she had a long wool overcoat slung over one arm.

"This was Carl's. Now it's yours. It has deep pockets. You'll need deep pockets."

After the paper-doll song ended, somber trumpet music heralded the start of the next program—one hosted by the Voice, his odd pauses and unusual emphases creating a distinctive cadence.

"This is Farley Sackstead in London. German troops continue to suffer heavy losses as the Russian army advances from the east, pushing the Nazis closer to their own borders…"

His voice had been very upsetting to the Cat Woman. She'd rushed across the room and scattered droplets of water onto the radio from a small vial, afterward dropping the empty container onto the floor where several cats went after it, batting the tiny cylinder about until it rolled under the burnt-out Barcalounger. "The war is ending," she'd submitted to Riley. "The Voice will come back to America. That's our chance." She'd next taken him to the basement and shown him how to manufacture cartridges for Carl's pistol, using her late husband's press to combine shells, gunpowder, primers, and projectiles. She'd given Riley a chance to make bullets too, but he'd struggled—forgetting one step and then another, wrestling with the intricacies of Carl's press, and eventually knocking over the cannister of gunpowder.

"It's too hard. You can't do it."

"I *can, too,* do it! I ain't stupid. I had trouble in boot with some stuff, but I could tuck in my bedroll till you could bounce a quarter on it…and I hit the bullseye on the range ninety times out of a hundred! I ain't stupid! I ain't no imbecile."

He'd managed to produce four bullets while the Cat Woman told him about the mission he was to undertake. Her plan had made him uneasy.

"Jenny might not like me doin' a thing like that."

"Yes, she will."

"I don't know. She—"

"Don't worry. When it's done, that girl will love you. I promise."

"'…that our flag was still there,'" Jenny sang as Riley again checked the huge clock at the rear of the stage. The thin hand was crossing over the *7* on its way to the *8*. One of the fat hands was nearly on the *6*, the other nudging the *12*. He remembered the Cat Woman's instructions.

"Wait until the fat hands connect the 12 and the 6."

His finger gently grazed the trigger of the gun in his pocket. For tonight's mission it was loaded with bullets he'd made after the Cat Woman let him try again, setting out the components, then patiently watching him add two more cartridges to his original four.

"'Oh, say does that…'" Jenny continued, the fat hands of the clock on the stage nearly straight up and down, the thin hand sweeping across the *8*. Twenty seconds remained until the old war was over and the new one began.

Antoni

"I'm all right," Antoni answered the major, breaking his silence as the voice of the girl on the radio competed with the drawling guard. The officer didn't press him, something Antoni appreciated. The American knew Antoni's history with Stangl and was sympathetic but not intrusive. He respected boundaries, unlike the drawling guard. A sergeant and a talker, the military policeman reminded Antoni of Janusz, the farmer who'd opened the door of his single-level home near the Polish-Ukrainian border on the morning after the uprising. Both men were big and rawboned. Neither much cared for Jews.

After fleeing the camp, Antoni had veered northeast through the forest, emerging just below a body of water too insignificant to merit a name. He'd then worked his way south, staying within the fringe of the woods until he came upon Janusz's farm. Worked by the big man's family for over a century, the property was large—over six hundred acres—and had managed to elude the war; the fields free of shell craters; the house, barn, and silo intact. It was past harvest, the cornstalks in the field nearest the house yellow and flattened, the tall silo adjacent to the barn filled nearly to the top with seed corn. Janusz, husky with broad features and big knuckles, had fashioned a sour face when he answered the knock on his farmhouse door and discovered a man in filthy camp stripes standing on his porch. He'd waved a hand as if shooing him off.

"Idź stad... Nie możemy ci pomóc." *Go away... We can't help you.*

Then a woman's voice had called out from inside the home.

"Kto to jest, Janusz?" *Who is it, Janusz?*

"Żyd...z obozu." *Jew...from the camp.*

A few moments later a wide-hipped woman with light hair and a lighter disposition had appeared at the big farmer's side. Nearly a foot shorter than her broad-shouldered bear of a husband, Tillie's eyes had momentarily widened at the sight of the Sobibor escapee. Then she'd stepped onto the porch, warily looking past Antoni to the red, yellow, and orange leaves that distinguished the edge of the autumn forest from the recently harvested cornfield abutting it.

"Come with me."

"We can't get involved, Tillie."

"He needs help, Janusz. We must help him."

"But he's a—"

"Hush! We must help."

The little woman had then pulled Antoni into a large room where kitchen, dining area, and parlor were incorporated into a single space. Burning logs popped and crackled within a huge fireplace on one wall, and three small girls—the oldest about ten—sat at a wide kitchen table, their eyes round at the sight of the bedraggled stranger. Tillie led Antoni to the table and made him sit.

"First you must eat a little. Then you must bathe. What is your name?"

"Antoni."

"Janusz, get Antoni fresh clothes…and put on water for a bath."

Another brief dispute between husband and wife had ensued, Janusz upset to be volunteered, Tillie making clear he'd been conscripted. Afterward she'd sent her younger two daughters outside to keep watch for German soldiers while ten-year-old Krsytyna piled kiełbasa alongside creamy quark cheese onto a slab of bread.

"That's too much," the girl's mother told her after Krystyna placed the food on the table. She'd divided the meal into thirds, putting one helping on a fresh plate.

"Start with this, Antoni…and eat slowly. Let your stomach get used to it."

After Antoni finished eating, Tillie ordered him to strip.

"Thank you, but I must go. My wife…I have to find—"

"You stink, Antoni. The Germans will smell you from a kilometer away. A bath, some sleep, and then you can look for your wife. Janusz will help you. Now take off those rags."

Antoni had hesitated, anxiously eyeing the farmwife's daughter, but Tillie hadn't been concerned.

"This is a farm, Antoni," she forwarded. "We have animals. Krystyna and I have seen a pecker before."

The feel of hot water on his skin for the first time in years had been soporific, Antoni struggling to stay awake after sinking into the tub. Eventually he'd given up—the warm bath, blazing fireplace logs, his full belly, and exhaustion allowing sleep to steal him.

"Shut up…and get out here, sergeant!" the American major suddenly yelled from the open doorway that connected the guardroom to the cellblock. It startled Antoni and ended a singing duel between the girl on the radio and the drawling guard. Antoni looked up. The major held Stangl's Luger in his hand. He'd reattached the silencer to the end of the barrel. A typically sober man, his face was unreadable, as if detachment could disguise the portent of the weapon.

"I've changed my mind," the major said. "I think you're right. Stangl will never talk. It's time to put him behind us."

He placed the gun on the bench next to Antoni along with a key.

"You understand don't you, Antoni? We're done with him. Best to put him behind you."

5

7 May 1945

1759:41 to 1759:50 Eastern Standard Time
2359:41 to 2359:50 Central European Time

Farley

"'Star-Spangled banner yet wave,'" the girl at center stage sang, adding a run and then a pause as she built to the finale. The sound engineer no longer pressed messages against the glass wall separating his cubicle from Farley's. Slouched in his chair, he indolently surveyed the crowd outside the booth as the journalist mulled over words to cap fifteen-year-old Jenny Doyle's rendition of the nation's national anthem. Farley had been moved by her performance, feeling an unexpected connection to the country from which he'd been so long disconnected. It was an emotion he believed was shared with the nation. War had provoked a sense of unity in the too often disunited United States. Farley had seen it among the troops on the battlefield, in an England battered by German rocket attacks, and upon his return to America with those who'd kept the home fires burning.

Patriotic spirit had proven to be infectious and it appeared that Antoni Pietkowski had been infected. "We want our child to be an American," he'd professed during Farley's interview with the Pietkowskis in Yorkshire. "We've been trying to arrange passage to America, but the British aren't cooperating. They want me to stay here and work for them." The earlier resurrection of Franz Stangl's name had sent Gosia out of the parlor, and after rejoining them she offered tepid agreement before apologizing for her earlier abrupt exit. Farley had quickly reassured her. "I should be the one apologizing. I've dredged up terrible memories for you. I'm very sorry."

After the interview Farley returned to London and made calls, then revisited Yorkshire a few weeks later, joined by a man from the American Judge Advocate General's Corps. The officer—a major—came with a visa for Gosia and an offer for Antoni. "There will be trials in Nuremberg for the men who committed war crimes," he told the couple. "We've already captured some of them and translators are needed. We'll catch the rest too." He'd hesitated, then added, "It's a chance for your child to be born in America... Perhaps a chance to help hang the bastards who ran the camps too."

A few weeks later Farley drove the Pietkowskis to an American airfield in England where Gosia climbed aboard a huge C-54 military cargo plane. Despite their imminent separation, the couple was grateful to the famous journalist for reaching out to the American army on their behalf. "I'm sure our baby will be a girl, but if it's a boy, we shall name him Farley," Gosia told him in Polish, a hand resting on her abdomen. After Antoni translated her words into English, the journalist laughed.

"Oh my goodness, Gosia, don't saddle your child with my name. If he's to be an American, I suggest something like Joe or Tom. Those are good names. Farley is the name you give someone when you want the other kids at school to break his glasses." It was meant to be a joke but after her husband translated Gosia hadn't laughed, instead offering an earnest response her husband forwarded to Farley in English.

"She says, 'Okay. If it is a boy, we shall name him Joe.'"

Outside the broadcast booth Jenny Doyle reached the penultimate lyric in the national anthem. "'Oh, say does that...'" she began, abruptly cutting herself off when the boy with dark, forbidding eyes shoved his way past the burly man in the front row of spectators. He pulled a gun from one pocket of his long, heavy overcoat and pointed it at the singer. Farley reflexively stood, watching as the gunman's arm swept across the stage and then stopped with his pistol aimed at the broadcast booth.

The veteran journalist had been in crosshairs before. A sniper at Anzio had just missed, his bullet ripping through the newsman's shoulder bag. He'd not even flinched, the incident over before he could consider his own mortality. But this time was different. There was no anonymity, no camouflage. This time Farley Sackstead looked directly into the eyes of the gunman.

The door on Farley's side of the glass enclosure suddenly opened and Nobbie Wainwright barged in, smelling of sweat and cigarettes, a faint red smudge on the collar of his otherwise white shirt. Farley pointed at the assassin. Nobbie followed his finger, his eyes widening when he saw the gun.

"Holy shit!"

The boy's finger tightened on the trigger of his pistol. Behind him the burly man in suspenders grabbed a fistful of his coat. And on the stage a fifteen-year-old girl from Queens, New York, abandoned the microphones, dashing for the front edge of the temporary platform erected in Times Square to celebrate V-E Day. Farley Sackstead watched it all, cataloguing the details as if he were once again a reporter for the *Chicago Tribune* and would have to write the story. Words for the lede instinctively formed, even as his heart pounded and he realized they would not be on page one but among the obituaries.

On 7 May 1945, journalist Farley Sackstead was assassinated in Times Square. His wife was right. His damned job finally killed him.

Selma

Growing up on East Fifty-Second Street when it was filled with houses, Selma had run everywhere, never falling. Her balance was perfect. Now as she left her porch with three vials of Miracle Holy Water in one pocket of her overcoat and her family Bible in the other, she worried about a fall and a broken hip if she ran from her ramshackle house to the building across the parking lot. Nevertheless, she broke into a trot as the voice of the girl singer blasted from the speakers attached to the CBS building.

"'Star-Spangled banner yet wave...'"

Before the radio network purchased the property for their headquarters, a few of the homes where the parking lot now resided had been sold to make way for a large stable. It had still been there when her parents died and Owen returned. She'd been happy to see her brother, happier that Father was dead and could no longer argue with his son. They'd argued all the time, the final dispute sending Owen away for good. "No son of mine will go to the Pope's college!" Father had roared when her brother told him about the school in Indiana. He'd been wrong. Owen had gone to Notre Dame and not returned while his parents were still alive.

Selma's father roared even louder a year later when she told him about the baby. She'd had to face her parents alone and still remembered her mother's silence, her father's belt, her suitcase on the sidewalk when she came home from school the next day.

I still remember things...not everything. But some things.

Selma kept her eyes on the second-floor window of the apartment building as she hurried across the CBS parking lot, praying for Riley to complete his mission before the infant was delivered—to dispatch the Voice before the beast could claim the Polish woman's child, just as he'd callously taken hers. Selma's son had arrived nearly four months too early those many years ago—a tiny creature born on a night when a harvest moon illuminated the sky in an orange glow, his arms and legs spindly, his head oddly shaped, his eyes widely spaced. He never tried to breathe and they'd whisked him away before she could hold him, allowing Selma merely a glimpse of his hairless, veiny head and dusky skin before a nurse rushed him off. "Taken care of, dear," was the answer given when the despondent mother later asked what had become of her child. "Barren," the doctor told her the next day when she wanted to know how long to wait before again trying.

I still remember things...

Carl had reacted to the loss with a shrug, the prospect of fatherhood as uninteresting to him after the birth as it had been before. "Wouldn'ta married you if I'd known this was gonna happen," he'd complained. He never again touched Selma, seeking comfort from other women until too little hair and too much belly put them off. Selma had subsequently lapsed into loneliness, followed by the strange and progressive madness doctors blamed on her cats. Five had shared their tiny apartment in the Lower East Side before Selma's miscarriage, their malodorous litter boxes scattered about. Ten more found a home with them after her parents died and they moved into the house on Fifty-Second Street. The dog kept the herd manageable while his master was alive, but after Carl died in his favorite chair, the dog absconded and dozens more cats had eagerly replaced him.

The cat disease had rendered Selma's balance unreliable, her vision blurred in a way that spectacles couldn't correct, and she struggled not to fall as she ran. Age hadn't helped. Selma wasn't sure how old she was. She'd once known. Older than sixty. The Bible in her pocket contained family birthdates, but the book had been on the side table next to Carl's vacant Barcalounger when lightning exploded into the living room and ignited the chair. The Bible had survived, but its leather cover was burned away, the underlying page with inscribed birthdates erratically charred. Carl had been dead more than a year by then, passing while cradled in his precious Barcalounger—head rolled back, mouth open. At first Selma had believed him deeply asleep, but after a few hours without his thunderous snores reverberating about the house or a cloud of toxic farts polluting the air, she'd pried open his half-lidded eyes and used a penlight to confirm nonreactive pupils.

From the speakers attached to the outside of the CBS building across the parking lot, the voice of the girl in Times Square resounded. The end of the anthem and the top of the hour both approached. Selma hoped Riley would remember.

"Wait…until the 12 is connected to the 6."

He was a good boy, a loyal boy. He tried. But he was dull-witted and didn't always remember. He struggled to learn and then to remember it. Selma had tried to teach him how to manufacture cartridges, but it hadn't worked out. The first time he'd spilled the can of gunpowder, the next time forgetting to add it altogether or improperly setting the casing in the press. "I ain't stupid," he'd huffed. "I can do it." But he couldn't, and before sending him off on his mission Selma had replaced the faulty cartridges he'd fashioned with ones she'd made.

But he knows his numbers. He knows to wait…until the 12 is connected to the 6.

Selma reached the door leading to the apartments above the deli and then stopped, trying to remember why she'd left her house to come there. She pulled the Bible from the pocket of her heavy overcoat and looked at it, praying for God to provide the answer. The leather cover was burned away save the edge closest to the binding, the facing page with birthdates browned from the heat of the long-ago fire. The entry that chronicled her birth was partially readable.

Selma Dorothy Sackstead: May 8, 188

Below her name was Owen's, his birthdate obscured, and then the only fully readable name and birthdate on the page. It belonged to Owen's son…Selma's nephew.

Farley Robert Sackstead: June 6, 1902

Jenny

"He's creepy," Bridget decided after Jenny described Riley Blaine. "Don't answer his letters if he writes."

"He never said anything about writing," Jenny had argued, feeling oddly protective of her brother's friend. "I'm not even sure he can write. Jimmy told me that he's…slow, you know? Has trouble learning stuff."

Bridget had been less sanguine. "He'll write…or show up on your doorstep. From what you told me, he's got eyes for you." She'd lifted an eyebrow, adopting the distinctive accent of movie vampire Bela Lugosi. "He vants to drink your bluhd."

Jenny had laughed, even though she wasn't amused. Riley's eyes had tracked her every move on his single night in the Doyle home, making her feel as if he did indeed want to steal her soul. To wrap himself around her. To absorb her. He'd professed his love from the steps of the railcar as it pulled away from the platform the next day, the exigence in his voice both puzzling and frightening.

"'Star-Spangled banner...'" Jenny sang as Riley Blaine squeezed past her father. He wore an oversized winter coat, even though the evening temperature was nearly sixty degrees, his face glistening with sweat as he stared at Jenny as if pleading, his eyes black as cinder and less filled with love than bereft of hope. One hand was shoved into a pocket of the heavy coat and Jenny shivered almost imperceptibly, suddenly visited by the feeling that someone was about to die.

She'd felt the same rush of foreboding on the morning her mother passed. Jenny had risen and dressed for school that day, afterward eating breakfast while reading the back of the Wheaties box, and then gathering her things. But when it was time to say goodbye and head for P.S. 146, Siobhan Doyle had hugged her more tightly than usual, holding on when Jenny tried to pull away.

"Mom! I gotta meet Bridget. I'm gonna be late!"

"Too old for your mom to hug?"

"Just leave me alone!"

On the way to school Jenny had almost turned around and gone back. But she hadn't. Bridget had been waiting at the corner with the latest issue of *Screenbook*. Robert Taylor and Hedy Lamarr were on the cover and Jenny had shrugged off the premonition. Afterward she and Bridget gushed over the handsome actor, parodied Lamarr's exotic accent, and went on to school. An hour later her mother slumped over the kitchen table, her heart giving out as she tried to figure out how to make ends meet with a husband who drank away too much of his paycheck and two children who would need to go to college or risk ending up like their parents. Later in the confessional, Jenny blamed herself for her mother's death. "You can't fix a weary heart," the priest had consoled her. But his absolution of her sin hadn't helped.

"'…yet wave…'" she sang, struggling to ignore Riley. His appearance at the front of the crowd threatened to send the lyrics of "The Star-Spangled Banner" flying off and she searched for someone safe to concentrate on—someone who would help her finish the song in less than one minute and twenty-two seconds, setting a new record for her father to brag about. Her eyes darted about, briefly resting on a pair of New York City cops standing beside a streetlight. One was ramrod straight, hat under his arm, a hand over his heart. The other was younger and had less reverence for the flag than a young woman in the crowd whose tight skirt hugged a round bottom. Jenny sensed movement to her right and glanced at the glass broadcast booth. A large man was entering the enclosure. The famous radio journalist, Farley Sackstead, had risen from his chair, his eyes on Riley. "'O'er the land…'" Jenny pressed on, following the journalist's gaze. Riley's hand was no longer in his pocket. It now held a gun. Pointed at her.

Most of the thousands gathered in Times Square were preparing for the final ten seconds of the countdown, watching the huge clock at the back of the stage, popping corks on champagne bottles brought to the impending celebration, or sizing up who they might kiss when the clock struck six p.m. Jenny stopped singing. Then someone near the stage screamed, the sound rippling backward from the leading edge of the amassed thousands. Riley began to rotate in a circle, the dignitaries seated behind Jenny recoiling in a wave as the barrel of the gun swept past them. He stopped with the weapon pointed at Farley Sackstead and Jenny left the microphones at center stage. The shouts and screams grew louder, but she didn't hear them, nor did she see the snotty production assistant run for cover nor Mayor LaGuardia's security men rush him off the stage. She didn't see her father grab a fistful of Riley's heavy coat from behind or the two cops by the lamppost brandish their nightsticks as they began to fight their way through the panicking spectators. Instead, fifteen-year-old Jenny Doyle from Queens, New York, saw only the gun with Riley Blaine's finger beginning to squeeze the trigger as she raced for the edge of the stage and then launched herself from it.

STANGL

Stangl couldn't push Gosia from his mind—her face, her breasts, the hair between her legs, the sound of her moans as he rammed himself into her. *Had she hidden in one of the haystacks they'd searched. Cowered in a barn loft? What if I had found her?* He'd shot a man for hiding a Jew. Executed as a warning to the others, the soldier had been a member of the regular German army. Stangl hadn't known his name, nor cared. "Karl Janning," his aide, Kurth, later reported. "A popular man, Hauptsturmführer…well thought of among the others. His best friend is Zimmer. They grew up together. Zimmer is engaged to marry his sister. Perhaps…"

"Perhaps what?"

"Zimmer should be re-posted?"

Stangl had been annoyed with Kurth for implying that he should fear his own men, hated even more that it was true. "You are not a likable man, Stangl," Himmler had once told him. "That is not a bad thing. I, too, am unlikable. But I am feared. Fear is preferable to likability. If your men fear you, they will do your bidding without question no matter how terrible the act you order them to perform." Himmler's advice and Kurth's impertinence had obligated Stangl to join Zimmer and Braun's squad on their next patrol. It proved to be a bad decision. On a farm five kilometers from the death camp at Sobibor, he'd dispatched Zimmer to search the barn, and when the young soldier didn't emerge after several minutes, Stangl went inside.

"What's taking so long, private? Hurry up!"

Well over a year had passed since that cold, dreary afternoon, but Stangl still remembered a world turned chillingly silent when Zimmer slowly brought his Mauser up to waist level, its barrel aimed at his commanding officer's heart. The SS officer had once presided over an execution by firing squad. The condemned, a Wehrmacht colonel, had acquitted himself well at the end. One of the sundry royals dominating the leadership ranks of the regular German army when Hitler came to power, he'd lived up to his legacy by dying bravely, his tunic fully buttoned, the blindfold spurned, a cigarette in a long ivory holder clenched between his teeth. "Gut zielen," he'd growled. *Aim well.*

Stangl had been impressed, resolving that he, too, would die bravely with "Sieg Heil!" on his lips and his family in his thoughts should he ever be lashed to a post. However, with Zimmer's gun pointed at him, the haughty SS officer hadn't lauded Hitler nor wished for a last kiss from his wife, Theresa, nor goodbye hugs from his three daughters. Instead, he'd lamented that the only woman he ever truly loved—Gosia Pietkowski—had once been accessible to him, yet unattainable. It was Gosia he'd visualized in what might have been his final seconds on Earth, silently bewailing the Jewish pedigree that prohibited her from joining him in the afterlife. His regret had been fleeting. Before the White Death's trembling legs sent him to his knees, Zimmer had lowered his weapon and spoken, his voice flat.

"I'm coming, Herr Hauptsturmführer."

"'Star-spangled banner...'" the girl on the radio sang, the slight hitch in her delivery inexplicably filling Stangl with the same dread he'd felt during those perilous moments in the Polish barn. Zimmer had been oddly dispassionate that day, despite the hatred he must have felt for his commanding officer, his lack of emotion more terrifying than the rage and vengefulness Stangl knew must have lurked below the surface. Such dispassion made the once-feared SS officer feel insignificant—as if he were a name on a list of casualties in the newspaper, a number on a report no one at high command would read, or a hiccup in the vast history of the universe—indeed, as if he were a Jew shuffling along in a line that led to Lager III.

"'O'er the land...'" the American girl on the radio sang as Stangl pondered the trial, conviction, and inevitable sentence that awaited him. They would claim that justice was served, but the outcome would be no more just than the execution of the Wehrmacht colonel who had bravely died because the cowards under his command failed to hold a bridge the Führer wanted held. The former SS officer's confiscated Luger had been on the American major's belt when he entered the cell with Antoni Pietkowski behind him. The flap of the holster had been unsecured, and for a few terrifying seconds, he'd feared Antoni might grab the gun and preempt the execution that undoubtedly awaited the former commandant at Sobibor. But he hadn't, and Stangl had been puzzled. The major wouldn't have stopped him. A hanging was in store anyway, an assassination saving the Americans the cost of a good rope.

The singer on the radio abruptly cut herself off, and as if it were a cue, Stangl was unexpectedly visited by a different explanation for Antoni's reluctance and the major's restraint. He smiled.

Perhaps Hudal has lined a high enough pocket?

Jimmy

"'Star-Spangled Banner...'" Jenny's voice streamed into a night otherwise quiet on the roadway cutting through the Lorenzer forest—no more snapped twigs, no hushed voices, no click of a rifle bolt slid into place. Cap had warned the crew to stay inside the fences after dark, worried that the war was still officially in progress despite an unofficial ceasefire. "More'n a few Jerries might want 'em an American scalp or two before they throw in the towel," he'd cautioned his men. Jimmy now wished he'd listened, even though none of the Germans who'd shown up outside the gates of Feucht Airfield had been scalp hunting. Their belts weaponless, their hands raised, their bellies empty, they'd been more interested in soup than scalps. Cleaned up and fed, they'd quickly learned enough English to trade their medallions and insignia for cigarettes and Hershey bars. Jimmy had wanted to hate them but couldn't, the German boys more like Americans than any of the Englishmen he'd known while stationed at High Wycombe. It was an argument he offered to Cap, but the West Virginian remained unconvinced. "Them boys comin' outta the woods been reg'lar army so far, Jimmy. Ain't none been SS. Them SS fellas is flat-out crazy. They ain't gonna crawl in here with tails 'tween their legs. They'll be lookin' to get even."

Stories of SS zeal and their atrocities had filtered across the Atlantic to the United States when Jimmy was still in high school. The unbridled inhumanity of Hitler's personal army had shocked the students at John Adams High, more than a few convinced that such behavior was peculiar to Germans. "Americans would never do such things," one of Jimmy's classmates asserted during an English class that had strayed from a discussion of retribution in *The Merchant of Venice*. Their teacher—a veteran who lost an arm in the Great War—promptly assigned the novella *The Ox-Bow Incident*, in which a posse hunts down and then lynches three alleged rustlers, only to later learn they've hanged innocent men. "It's a cautionary tale," he'd soberly informed his class, explaining how the author, Walter van Tilburg Clark, wanted to show his readers that the urge to embrace fascism was not confined to Nazi Germany. "A lynch mob like we've had in this country, and still have in parts of the United States, is just fascism in a bottle cap," he'd suggested to his students. "It proves that no one, not even Americans, are above succumbing to some version of Adolf Hitler."

Jimmy peered into the darkness, trying to make out shapes. With the unofficial end of hostilities, most of the regular German army troops had simply put down their weapons and made for home. However, the *Daisy Mae* and its bomber wing had destroyed twenty percent of the housing in 150 cities. One of the most devastated was nearby Nuremberg, which had been reduced to a collection of skeletal buildings and rubble-filled streets. Someone from Nuremberg might have discovered a bomb crater where his home once stood, Jimmy considered, and was now more interested in payback than capitulation.

He wouldn't be alone in that.

By the end of their bombing runs, the *Daisy Mae*'s missions had reached deep into Germany, rumors abounding that downed and captured Allied airmen were summarily executed, often by civilians enraged by errant bombs intended for armament factories that had landed on their homes and shops. Like the rest of the crew, Jimmy had pretended the rumors didn't worry him, boasting he'd fight rather than give up. "Gonna get killed anyway," he bragged to English girls in the pub. "Might as well take a few Krauts with me." Now, in the dark, the boast seemed vainglorious—not the oath of a man who might have a Mauser trained on him but that of a boy playing army with a cap gun.

Jimmy cautiously lifted his head and peered into the forest. No gunshot rang out. No more movements disturbed the night, and he calculated the odds that something with four legs rather than two was above the road. Even if it were a German, he reasoned, he was probably looking for a meal and a bunk, afraid to call out lest he got himself shot before he could surrender.

That's gotta be it…just wants to surrender.

Jimmy took a deep breath, released it, and then slowly rose from the cover of the high grass, Cap's .45 held level at his waist. Nothing happened and he carefully eased the hammer down, then lowered his arm until his weapon was pointed at the ground. At the same time a slender beam of moonlight slipped between the branches of the trees, casting him into soft light.

Just seeing things…losing my marbles.

Another twig snapped and Jimmy dropped to a knee, his weapon pointed at the sound.

"Who's there?" he shouted. "Show yourself."

Gosia

To reach America, Gosia had boarded a C-54 cargo plane filled with returning soldiers, the cold, crowded aircraft reminding her of the barracks at Sobibor, the American GIs packed into the giant ship too much like their German counterparts: all broad shoulders and ribald laughter. However, once they were in the air and she began to have contractions the men shushed one another, hanging tarps to create a private chamber in the aft section of the huge plane. One of the soldiers was a first-generation Polish-American from Omaha. "You remind these boys of home...of their wives and girlfriends," he'd explained in her native tongue. "Some have babies they've never held."

The transport had been arranged by the American journalist Farley Sackstead, after he traveled to Yorkshire for an interview with two survivors of the uprising at Sobibor. He'd been accompanied by a Polish expatriate and fighter pilot, Nowak, who'd flown with the RAF since the Battle of Britain and was fluent in English. Sackstead had surprised Gosia, looking more like a librarian than a world-famous radio newsman. Nowak, however, had looked exactly like the combat pilot he was—a flinty-eyed man with rumpled skin along one side of his neck. He hadn't been offended when Gosia stared at his scars. "Burned," he told her in Polish. "Didn't bail out fast enough." He'd remained even after learning that Antoni spoke perfect English, studying the couple—particularly Antoni—as if the interview were for a job rather than a radio piece.

The session had occupied most of the afternoon with Sackstead asking open-ended questions that invited exposition:

Did you have any idea what was waiting for you at Sobibor?
What was a typical day like?
How was the camp organized?
How did the plan for the uprising begin?

Antoni had provided most of the answers, Gosia sitting quietly as her husband calmly recalled the ghetto in Warsaw and the cattle-car train ride to Sobibor with two queues on arrival—one to the workers' barracks, the other to the chambers. With Sackstead recording his voice and taking notes, Antoni had described the layout of the camp: Lagers I and II for workers, Lager III for the condemned. He recounted the plan for the uprising that languished until the Russian Red Army soldier Pechersky came to the camp and described the day of the revolt: how he'd split Nieman's skull with an axe, shot a tower guard, battered another to death, and then dashed across and around corpses on the minefield. He told Sackstead about Janusz and Tillie and their three daughters; about the miraculous discovery of Gosia in the forest; their months on the farm; the Germans' retreat; the couple's flight west from advancing Russians; and the elements of the Polish Home Army they'd stumbled upon and fought with. Antoni explained how they'd come to be housed with a host family in Yorkshire. "We met a British military advisor attached to the Polish army. He wanted me to work for their intelligence service after the war. He was the one who arranged for Gosia and me to come here."

Soon thereafter the story of the Pietkowskis' harrowing escape from Sobibor aired on the journalist's radio broadcast, making Antoni and Gosia both celebrated and notorious in their tiny Yorkshire village—some sympathetic to the epic saga, others preferring for Jews to live elsewhere. A month later Sackstead returned with the major, the American army officer bringing a visa for Gosia and work for Antoni as a translator. Gosia could go to America, the major told them, but Antoni would have to be in Germany for at least a year or more. After the two men were gone, Gosia begged her husband to reject the offer.

"It will never be safe for us in Germany."

"You won't be there, dearest. You'll be in the United States."

"I don't want to be in America without you. I don't want us to be apart… Ever again."

A few days later Gosia changed her mind after Nowak returned, bringing along a man from the Jewish Agency who shared his ambitions for an internationally recognized homeland in Palestine. "You're right, Antoni. I'll go to America. You can join us later," she'd encouraged her husband after the men left, calculating that a wife and child in the land of milk and honey would discourage Antoni from joining the Zionist leader in his dangerous enterprise. Now she wondered if her strategy had been wrong. After more than two months in the United States, she hadn't seen much, if any, milk and honey.

"'O'er the land...'" the girl on the radio continued as Gosia's contraction continued to build. Suddenly and for the first time in more than an hour she sensed movement, the baby's head slightly lower in her pelvis.

"On próbuje," she cried out. *He's trying.*

"She shouldn't push anymore," Rita, the midwife, groused to Gosia's aunt. "She needs a C-section." Ewa asked for more explanation and then translated the response for her niece.

"An operation?" Gosia said in Polish.

Her aunt nodded, her face sober.

"I'll call an ambulance," Rita told Ewa. "Where's your phone?"

"On próbuje," Gosia protested.

"No more pushing!" Rita snapped at her, looking at Ewa. "Tell her!"

"On próbuje!" Gosia repeated.

"She's gonna kill the baby. Tell her to stop!"

"On próbuje...on próbuje!"

Zimmer

"'Star-Spangled banner...'" the distant voice of the American singer resonated as she built to the coda of her song. Zimmer hoped her countryman on the roadway below was listening, that he'd been distracted or perhaps blamed the sharp snap of the twig on an animal predator rather than what Zimmer had become: prey. It was ironic. Once the hunter of defenseless fugitives after the uprising at Sobibor, the unarmed Wehrmacht soldier was now the hunted—unarmed, vulnerable, perhaps about to be discovered.

This is how they felt.

He'd found them on a farm near the Ukrainian border. After scaling a ladder to the top of a grain silo, he'd opened the hatch and peered inside just as two heads emerged from an irregular surface of seed corn two meters below him. Most of the fugitives after the death camp revolt had headed west toward the interior of Poland, but the pair inside the silo had gone southeast toward Ukraine. It had been a smart move, Zimmer conceded at the time. Hauptsturmführer Stangl's SS officers were cowards who didn't relish an encounter with Red Army troops, leading their regular German army men on abbreviated searches of the areas east of the camp, their eyes warily scanning the horizon for Soviet soldiers. Stangl's weasel of an aide, Untersturmführer Kurth, had been in command of Zimmer's squad when they reached the farmstead that day, the vicious little SS worm more impatient than usual, urging his troops to hurry as he nervously paced about the farmstead, leering at the farmer's wife while wolfing down the kolaches she offered. Braun had voiced what they all thought.

"Bastard is worried he'll have to face someone who can shoot back."

They'd searched the house, barn, and chicken shed, leaving the silo for last.

"Private Zimmer," Kurth then ordered. "Climb up there and look inside."

Zimmer had once climbed to the top of the silo on his grandfather's farm only to find it crawling with rats inside the enclosure. Terrified, he'd lost his grip and fallen, breaking his arm. Afterward he'd had nightmares for years and the memory made him hesitate, shuddering almost imperceptibly. Braun had sensed his friend's dismay and offered to carry out the command. However, the scent of fear was as pungent to Kurth as skunk spray, and he'd repeated his order with a snake's smile curling his lips.

"I gave you an order, Private Zimmer! Get up there!"

From above the road to the airbase, Zimmer studied the patch of grass that now sheltered the American. *It's a stalemate*, he thought, recalling his chess matches with Karl Janning. As boys, they'd learned about stalemates and chess from Karl's father, playing with wooden pieces carved to depict characters from the Germanic legend of King Rother. Karl had won the initial battles with his friend. However, Zimmer's patience and talent for intrigue and strategy helped him catch up, and the boys had subsequently squared off in many hours-long battles that often ended in a stalemate. Karl's younger sister, Ilse, had typically been nearby during the boys' matches, shyly watching her brother's friend scrutinize the chessboard. At first Zimmer hadn't noticed her. But after she turned sixteen with long blond hair and porcelain features, he couldn't *stop* noticing her, losing game after game to her brother before finding a way to concentrate on the board rather than the straw-haired beauty with the vivid blue eyes. Zimmer and Ilse had fallen in love and agreed to marry after he finished university. Then the war came.

After receiving notice of her brother's death, Ilse had written Zimmer, begging for an explanation. Zimmer hadn't offered one on paper. Letters to and from Wehrmacht troops were carefully screened and censored, suspicious or disloyal passages referred to the Gestapo for further investigation. Such missives were dangerous to both writer and recipient, and Zimmer had waited until he was home on leave to tell Ilse and her parents that the cause of Karl's death had been a conscience. "He tried to be a hero," he told them. "And he was."

From the loudspeakers in the distance, the young American woman continued to sing, her voice replacing the memory of Ilse's peach complexion and full lips. "'…yet wave,'" she sang, the lyric delivered with a perceptible hitch; almost as if the girl had seen something disturbing in her faraway New York City audience. Zimmer wished it were daytime. In sunlight he could approach with his hands up. The American would see that he was unarmed and emerge from cover to accept his former enemy's surrender. Instead, the two men waited and wondered.

Suddenly the man on the roadside rose to his feet in the knee-high grass of the shoulder. Revealed by dull moonlight that filtered between the branches of the trees, his head was cocked as if to better listen, his handgun held at waist level like the gunslingers Zimmer had seen in American western movies.

After a few moments he lowered his arm, allowing the weapon to dangle at his side.

"Ich gebe auf," Zimmer murmured. "I give up."

He took a deep breath and ended the stalemate, stepping into the open with his hands raised. His boot found another dry branch. A sharp snap disrupted the night and the American instantly dropped to one knee, pointing his weapon at the sound. At the same time the girl on the radio stopped singing as if she, too, had spotted Zimmer standing outside the tree line, exposed in the same wedge of moonlight that illuminated what might be, at least for a few more seconds, an enemy soldier. The American called out, his words in English. Zimmer didn't answer, afraid that the only move he had left would result in checkmate.

Riley

"'Star-spangled banner…'" Jenny Doyle sang as Nobbie Wainwright reached the top of the stairs and then entered the glass-walled broadcast booth at the side of the stage. An hour earlier Riley had watched Nobbie and the redhead reenter the CBS building, then slipped in behind them. Following the Cat Woman's plan, he'd gone directly to the stairwell.

"*Stay off the elevator… It's a trap.*"

After quietly padding up the steps to the third-floor studio, he'd heard excited voices, cracked open the stairwell door, and seen Nobbie and the young woman atop a large desk with the CBS logo on the wall behind them. The redhead's dress was pulled up. Nobbie's pants were down.

"That's what you want, baby. That's what you want!"

"Yes, yes, yes!"

He remembered the same words coming from Mom's bedroom when Pap was on the Lakes. Five years old, he'd followed the grunts and moans to her bedroom. He'd seen Pastor Wondercheck's bare buttocks between his mother's widespread legs.

"*That's what you want!*"

"*Yes, yes!*"

Mom had been happy and mostly nice to him back then, turning sad and mean after the treacherous clergyman decided to abandon her. She'd salved her heartbreak with food and hatred of life with Riley and Riley's father, dying unreconciled to love lost. Repeatedly spurned but never giving up, she'd faithfully attended church services every Sunday until her death, sitting in the front pew where she openly pined for a man who made too much eye contact with the other women in his flock, ignoring her even though she sang louder than any of them.

"'Onward Christian soldiers...'"

Sitting in the stairwell with his back to the door Riley had waited until Nobbie and the redhead finished up with a high-pitched squeal from one and a lowing groan from the other. Afterward he'd heard muffled voices, followed by the sound of the elevator doors opening and closing, and then the hum of the car as it descended. After it stopped with a distant clank on the ground level, he'd cautiously looked out. The desk was tidy, the blotter straight, the telephone and file holder in place, the watchful eye of the CBS logo ostensibly blind to what had transpired. He'd next found the studio, using the large *L* the Cat Woman had inscribed in ink on the back of his hand.

"Stand in front of the big eye. The hand with the L will point at the studio. The Voice will be there."

But the Voice hadn't been there. The studio was deserted, save a very fat man alone in the ON AIR booth, feet propped up on a desk as he leaned back in his chair, a cloud of smoke hovering in the air around him. He'd not seemed concerned at the sudden appearance of someone brandishing a gun, taking a long drag from his cigarette and then luxuriously exhaling.

"What's la pistola about, amigo?"

"Where's the Voice?"

"Who's the Voice?"

"He comes on at seven o'clock 'cept tonight. Tonight, he's earlier."

"You talking about *This is London*?"

"He comes on at seven o'clock except tonight. Tonight—"

"Yeah, I get it, kid," the fat man interrupted. "Tonight, he's earlier. You're talking about Farley Sackstead. He's not here. You're in the wrong place. Your... *Voice*? He's in Times Square." He'd taken another deep drag from his cigarette then, holding it for several seconds before exhaling a cloud of bluish smoke. "Happy V-E Day," he'd added as Riley dashed from the studio, afterward running the entire ten blocks that separated the CBS Building from Times Square. He'd arrived out of breath but in time, the *12* and the *6* on the huge clock at the back of the stage not yet perfectly aligned.

"'...yet wave...'" Jenny sang as Riley more tightly gripped the gun inside the deep pocket of his coat. Jimmy had promised that she was the sweetest girl in the world and she had been, linking her arm in Riley's as she steered him through the crowds at the train station, talking nonstop as if she were his real girlfriend and not laughing when he later confessed his love for her. He remembered. It was a memory. Pastor Wondercheck believed that imbeciles didn't have memories, but they did. He could remember.

"I ain't stupid," Riley murmured. "I ain't no imbecile."

He'd told the Cat Woman about Jenny. "She'll see your picture in the newspaper," the old woman promised him. "She'll hear them talk about you on the radio." He would be God's warrior, someone admired and respected and loved. Someone Jenny could love.

Riley pushed past the large man in the front row, pulling the gun from his pocket, his eyes on the huge clock at the rear of the dais. The *12* was connected to the *6*. It was time. He was ready.

"'O'er the land...'"

From behind him the large man called out, his voice familiar.

"Run, Jenny!"

More shouts erupted, coalescing into a single wall of noise as people recoiled in horror, forming a clear halo on the street around him. Riley swung his arm through the air until his gun was pointed at the glass booth. The Voice was on his feet, talking into his microphone.

"'Onward Christian soldiers...'"
Riley squinted down the barrel of the gun, sighting his target.
"'...marching as to war.'"
Someone grabbed his coat from behind.
"'With the cross of Jesus...'"
He squeezed the trigger.
"'...going on before.'"

Antoni

The cellblock door remained open, the Luger and key to Stangl's cell on the bench. Antoni eyed the handgun. Before Sobibor he'd never touched a firearm but had used one of the smuggled rifles to shoot a tower guard during the uprising. A bolt-action Mauser with a capacity of five rounds, it had taken all five to hit the German watchman—the first three missing the turret altogether, the fourth splintering the rail atop the structure's wooden balustrade. It caught the sentry's attention and he'd aimed his machine gun at Antoni, the Mauser's fifth round hitting him between the eyes before he could unleash a torrent of bullets. Afterward Antoni used the empty weapon to bludgeon a pursuing guard, then tossed it aside and sprinted for the safety of the trees as bullets kicked up dirt around him and the slower or less lucky among the escapees fell.

The morning after he stumbled onto their farm Antoni awoke before first light. Janusz and Tillie were already up and they all sat at the kitchen table, drinking strong coffee as the Sobibor fugitive told them about the daring escape: the plan for a tunnel, the arrival of Pechersky, the chaos at the end. He didn't tell them about the three men he'd killed, worried the farm couple might be nonchalant about death when wringing a chicken's neck for the pot but perhaps less impassive about a murderer sharing coffee at their kitchen table.

"Pechersky promised to get Gosia out. We were to meet up later if I made it," he'd told the farm couple. They'd shared a look and then Tillie reached out to touch Antoni's hand.

"The Russians came through here, Antoni. Your man, Pechersky, was with them. There was no woman."

"Did he say anything about Gosia…if she made it out?"

"He didn't say much at all. They demanded food and clothes…threatened us if we didn't help."

"Goddamned Russians," Janusz had added. "They're all the same."

The big farmer had been convinced that Gosia was killed trying to escape, but Tillie insisted he help Antoni search for her anyway. "From what little they said, it seems the Russians didn't wander around like you," Janusz told Antoni after his wife blistered away his protests from behind the closed door of their bedroom. "They headed along a straight line that connects Ukraine to the camp, so if your wife was supposed to follow him she might be somewhere along that line."

They'd set out at daybreak, Janusz carrying a shotgun, Antoni armed with an ax. Janusz led the way until the forest closed around them. Then he made Antoni take the point. "She's your wife," he'd gruffly justified. "If one of us is to be shot, it should be you."

It had been a cloudy day and the woods thick, the position of the sun difficult to ascertain. Antoni had almost immediately become disoriented, but Janusz knew the forest bordering his farm as well as his shaggy herd dog knew her whelps. He'd grudgingly retaken the lead and not long thereafter they heard Gosia's voice, then saw her standing next to a huge tree, brushing dirt and twigs off her bottom. With the sound of their footsteps, she'd turned and pointed a rudimentary knife at them. Then she was in Antoni's arms, clinging to him so fiercely it was as if she wanted to turn them into a single thing that could never again be torn apart.

"'Star-Spangled Banner yet wave…'" the girl on the radio sang, a three-beat pause signaling that her song was nearly finished. Antoni knew the American anthem was meant to inspire—an homage to liberty and a life free of tyrants—but he was not moved. Tyrants were everywhere, tyranny sometimes confined to a single town or even a solitary expression of disgust.

Why will America be any different?

He picked up the key from the bench, then the gun. The preferred sidearm of Waffen-SS officers, the Luger's barrel was dark with oil, the grip cross-hatched, the unique silencer adding unexpected weight. Stangl had once pressed the barrel of the weapon against Antoni's forehead and then pulled the trigger. The hollow click when the hammer hit an unloaded chamber had buckled Antoni's knees, something Stangl found enormously amusing.

"Hast du dich vollgeschissen, drekig Juden?" *Did you shit yourself, dirty Jew?*

Antoni rose from the bench and moved into the cellblock, at the same time releasing the safety on the Luger. Inside, two rows of metal doors faced each other, three on each side, all solid save a view slit with a sliding panel. A single bare bulb hung from the ceiling, casting dull light that dissipated as it flowed into the shadowed corners. Stangl was the stockade's only prisoner. There was no sound coming from his cell.

"'O'er the land…'" the girl on the radio sang, suddenly cutting herself off, the unexpected silence allowing the American major's words to echo inside Antoni's head.

"Best to put him behind you."

"Diesmal, Herr Hauptsturmführer?" he softly murmured, the sickening memory of Gosia beneath a rutting, sweaty Stangl suddenly vivid. "Diesmal, wer wird sich selbst bescheißen."

This time, Captain…this time, who will shit himself?

6

7 May 1945

1759:51 to 1800:00 Eastern Standard Time
2359:51 to 2400:00 Central European Time

Farley

On the other side of the glass wall the engineer hid under his desk, while inside Farley's cubicle, Nobbie Wainwright was frozen in place, staring at the assassin as if the dark eye of the gun barrel could make him invisible. Farley was more contemplative than afraid, regretting that he wouldn't have a chance to say goodbye to Marta. He loved his wife and felt guilty for his dedication to a job that had separated them for so long. Before the war they'd shared a life filled with adventure and serendipities, visiting India and China and Africa, beginning a long friendship with Marlene Dietrich after meeting her on the Orient Express, and sharing a home one summer in Spain with classical guitarist Andres Segovia. They'd tried but were unable to have children, and with his parents no longer alive, Marta was the only family Farley had left unless one counted the aunt who lived less than a mile from where he now stood.

Upon his return from London he'd been surprised to see Aunt Selma's house still perched on one corner of the parking lot behind CBS headquarters; indeed, that morning he'd considered stopping by after his production meeting. But he hadn't, the home's tumbledown condition and the winter coat curiously dangling from a wire hanger on the front porch suggesting that madness lurked inside. He'd met her only once, traveling to New York from Indiana in 1919 after the house belonging to grandparents he'd never known passed through probate to

Aunt Selma and his father. His aunt and her boorish husband had already moved in from their Lower East Side apartment and he remembered her as a woman who might have been pretty with any effort at all. She'd been a midwife back then and taught midwifery as well. She'd loved cats, and as nearly as Farley could tell, hated her husband. It hadn't taken long for Farley to agree with her. Uncle Carl was a bigoted blowhard. He hated Italians, Jews, the Irish, Black people, Puerto Ricans, and Bolsheviks. He hated bus drivers, cabbies, Democrats, and Aunt Selma's cats. He liked beer and his dog. While Farley's father and Aunt Selma discussed what to do with the house and rental building, Uncle Carl had dragged Farley down to the basement, a cold, damp space made more inhospitable by his uncle's toxic farts. "There's gonna be a race war one o' these days and I'll be ready," he'd boasted, brandishing a pistol loaded with homemade cartridges, a finger dangerously curled around the trigger.

Inside the CBS broadcast booth, Farley began to speak into his microphone, his voice steady.

"A young man has emerged from the crowd—"

The gunman pulled the trigger before he could finish, his aim disrupted when Jenny Doyle piled into him after leaping off the edge of the stage. Sparks and smoke erupted from the barrel of the gun. A split-second later the bullet hit the wall of the broadcast booth and passed through, making a sound like a pebble hitting a car windshield. It didn't shatter the glass, instead leaving a tiny hole with stippled edges. An instant later a dull splat reverberated about the tiny cubicle when the slug hit Nobbie Wainwright in the center of his forehead.

Over the years a number of people had referenced Nobbie's muleheadedness when trying to spread a thin veneer of truth on one of his bombastic opinions. He was the king of pointed fingers, blaming Roosevelt for the Great Depression, crooked umpires for allowing the spit-balling Yankees to defeat his beloved Brooklyn Dodgers in the 1941 World Series, and Kathryn Hepburn's performance in *Woman of the Year* for encouraging

Nobbie's second and least annoying of three wives to divorce him. Thus it came as no surprise when the next day's news revealed what many had long suspected.

Not even a bullet could penetrate Nobbie Wainwright's thick skull.

As the crowd outside coalesced around and then swallowed the fallen gunman and young Jenny Doyle, the big ex-sportscaster wobbled slightly, a thin stream of blood dribbling down his nose from a wound between his bushy eyebrows. Then he abruptly crumpled to the floor of the broadcast booth, making a hollow sound when his head hit the bare wooden planks. At the same time the second hand on the huge clock at the back of the stage reached the *12*. A whistle sounded, followed by a pop, and a moment later the sky outside the booth turned red, white, and blue as crepe paper streamers and confetti were released from the roofs of buildings bordering Times Square. They fluttered earthward, filling the air and then sticking to the hair and clothes of the massive throng. Most of those present didn't know a gun had been fired, that Nobbie Wainwright had been wounded, that Jenny Doyle and the gunman were now buried in a gigantic dogpile, or that Farley Sackstead had figuratively dodged another bullet without literally dodging at all. Instead, they celebrated. It was V-E Day: 1800 hours on 7 May 1945 in New York City and midnight, May 8th, across the Atlantic in Germany. The war in Europe was over.

Selma

Selma's hips ached from the run across the parking lot as she limped up the uncarpeted steps that led to the apartments above the delicatessen. The stairway was long and narrow. She remembered climbing it with Father, feeling as if the walls were about to close in and crush her as she neared the top.

"Come with me. I need your help with something."

The first time, he'd called her away from her part-time duties as a shopgirl in the family shoe store. Working after school and on Saturdays, she was especially good with children and planned to become a nurse, then work with pediatric patients. "An excellent student... Definitely college material," the school counselor had advised her parents. "She has a chance to really make something of herself." Then Owen left and not long thereafter Father needed his daughter in the studio apartment above the ground-level shoe store. She was fifteen years old.

"Come with me. I need your help..."

Selma reached the second-floor door to apartment A, a suite composed of what had once been two apartments: a two-bedroom flat and the studio. A Jewish couple—the Dworaks—had leased both spaces for more than six years. They were good tenants, paying their rent for the store and their apartment on time, unlike many of Selma's other lodgers. They'd converted the former shoe store into a delicatessen, and the space once smelling of leather and shoe polish was now redolent of deli meats and cheeses. Selma visited the establishment every day, each time reminding the Dworaks that cat experimentation would not be tolerated. Mister Dworak was a bear of a man with kind eyes and hair everywhere: on his arms and neck, in his ears and nose. He spoke quietly, listened without interrupting, and added an extra pickle to the sandwiches she ordered. His wife was a tiny woman who nevertheless seemed large.

Carl had collected the rents while he was still alive, insisting the Dworaks pay with cash rather than a check like the other tenants. "Can't trust Jews," he'd contended, the cash somehow never finding its way into the account book. After he died the Dworaks were the only people to attend his funeral other than Selma. Mrs. Dworak brought food to Selma for days afterward and now the landlord accepted checks for their rent payments. The pregnant girl with eyes rimmed in sadness had shown up some weeks earlier, helping out in the delicatessen during peak hours. Perched on a high stool with unease draping over her like a funeral pall, she managed the cashbox while her aunt and uncle filled orders. At their first encounter she'd recoiled when Selma tried to touch her pregnant abdomen.

"She was in one of the camps," the girl's aunt explained.

"She's nervous...with new people." The girl and her aunt had exchanged a few words in Polish, the young woman then allowing Selma to put a hand and then an ear against her belly. Afterward Selma offered an assessment. "Good heartbeat... Fundal height consistent with about thirty-two weeks. The baby is fully formed. Just needs to put on some fat."

From the corridor, Selma heard voices through the apartment A door. Both belonged to women, one of them Mrs. Dworak, the other one angry.

"Push!"

"Suka!"

"Push!"

"Suka!"

The young Polish woman suddenly cried out.

"Nie moge!"

"Don't shout! Just push!"

Anger had surrounded Selma's labor too. "What did you expect when you spread your legs like a whore?" the midwife had berated her. "Stop crying and push!" She was only seventeen years old and the paternity was uncertain, visits with Father to the second-floor studio coinciding with reluctant sex in the back seat of Carl's car. Unlike the Polish girl, she'd not carried her child to term or even thirty-two weeks, the baby coming much earlier. Too early.

She'd endured her confinement alone, Carl in a bar down the street from the hospital, her parents ensconced in Lutheran judgment on East Fifty-Second Street. The baby inside her had been dead for a week, the effort to deliver the lifeless infant spanning two shifts of nurses, none interested in a teenager whose womb no longer harbored a heartbeat. They'd mostly left her alone, the midwife intuitively materializing when it was time to evict the baby.

"What did you expect when you spread your legs like a whore? Stop crying and push!"

"Push!"

"Suka!"

"Push!"

"Suka!"

Selma put an ear against the door of the apartment, then opened it and stepped inside. The Polish girl lay on her back at the end of the bed, her aunt at her side, a third woman standing between her legs. A radio was on the dresser. The Voice was speaking.

"A young man has emerged from the crowd—"

A muffled pop cut him off and Selma smiled.

Riley's done it!

"Mrs. Filbert?"

Selma looked at the woman standing at the end of the bed. Her eyes were wide, her lips parted. She looked surprised…and familiar.

I trained her…Rhonda? Rhoda? No…Rita.

Selma retrieved one of the vials of Miracle Holy Water from the pocket of her long overcoat. "You can go now, Rita," she said, holding up the vial. "I'm here."

"What?"

"You're not needed anymore."

The young Polish woman on the bed issued a low moan, her eyes searching the room as if seeking an escape.

"You can go," Selma reiterated to Rita. "I'm here."

Jenny

When later asked by reporters what she was thinking as she threw herself onto the gunman, Jenny would claim ignorance. But it wasn't true. She did remember. She thought about Jimmy when she deserted the microphones, thought about a letter he'd written as she made for the edge of the stage and then leapt from it. Her brother had rarely revealed much about the war when he wrote, but in one missive described what it felt like to be stuck inside a Plexiglas bubble on the underside of the *Daisy Mae* with German fighters buzzing about like murderous hornets and artillery shells exploding in the air like deadly kernels of popped corn.

Guess what, sis? Farley Sackstead from CBS radio was here to interview us because we're about to break a record for most missions in a B-17. He asked what it felt like when we were on a bombing run—what we thought about. The strange thing is that none of us could exactly remember. Cap told him that we weren't scared. "We don't think about what might happen," he told Mr. Sackstead. "Far as dying goes, we don't give a damn." He was right, Jenny. On a mission I never think about dying. I don't think, period. None of us do. Cap flies the plane, our bombardier, Lawson, drops the bombs, I aim and fire my 50s until there's nothing left to aim and fire at. I don't think about dying. I don't even care. It's like Cap said. We just don't give a damn. If we get killed, at least we'll be able to sleep past reveille.

Jenny landed on Riley as his weapon discharged, the gun making a sputtering sound rather than a sharp report. Riley crashed onto the concrete, Jenny atop his back. She lifted her head. There was a discrete hole in the glass of the CBS booth, a tiny perimeter of crushed fragments circumscribing it. The famous broadcaster, Farley Sackstead was still standing but no longer spoke into his microphone. The large man next to him was motionless, his arms dangling loosely at his sides, a trickle of blood dripping from the end of his nose. Suddenly the bloodied fellow collapsed and then the glass booth, the stage, and the sky disappeared as the space around Jenny and Riley contracted and they were swallowed by the crowd.

Everywhere were feet and knees. She heard cursing and the sounds of fists against chins. Bodies fell on and around them, the amassed weight pinning her to Riley and Riley to the concrete. The shrill sound of a whistle pierced the air, followed by a loud pop, and then a cascade of red, white, and blue streamers clouded Times Square, a few slipping through to join Jenny and Riley on a street littered with cast-off candy wrappers and cigarette butts.

"Get the gun!"

"Get him!"

"Get *off*!"

Jenny couldn't breathe, her eyes darting about, searching for a way out from under the bodies that continued to pile on.

Please...

More weight piled on. More air deserted her lungs.

"Get the gun!"

"Get him!"

"Get *off*!"

Jenny had heard the horror stories: people caught in a mad, panicked crowd and crushed to death.

It's not that. They'll get off. Someone will help.

But no one did. She tried to move but couldn't. Tried to breathe but couldn't.

Someone, please help.

She prayed, confessed, bargained, panicked, grieved.

Dear God...please help me.

Suddenly she was angry—angry with God for ignoring her and with Mrs. Petroff who had persuaded her to try out for MacPhail, Topping, and Webb. She was angry that someone at Yankee Stadium on that September night had been important enough to pick her to reprise "The Star-Spangled Banner" at the Times Square celebration. She was angry with the production assistant who was such a bitch and with Riley for precipitating the melee and with the selfish jerks about to squash the life from her under their combined weight. Last of all, she was angry with Jimmy.

I don't think about dying. I don't even care. It's like Cap said. We just don't give a damn.

How could he not care? They were both teenagers, their futures not privileges but promises. Jenny *did* care and now regretted abandoning the microphones and flinging herself off the stage, trying to be as brave as stupid Jimmy Doyle who was at last safe somewhere in Europe while his sister was about to be stampeded to death in America.

Jenny squirmed, pulled an arm free, and then pushed against the street with one hand until able to take a breath. Her effort allowed Riley to roll onto his back and face her. His lips moved, forming words without sound.

I love you, Jenny.

He pulled his arms free, put them across her shoulders, then pushed on the body above her as if lifting a barbell. It allowed them both to take shallow breaths.

"I love you," Riley repeated, his face so close it was a blur. This time she heard him.

The weight atop them lessened slightly as bodies began to peel off. She heard her father.

"Get off! You're crushing my daughter! Get off!"

More weight came off and Jenny was able to lift her head enough to put Riley in focus. He peered at her as if waiting for instructions, his eyes soft and innocent.

"Get us out of here, Riley," she said.

He didn't respond, instead wriggling back onto his belly. A patch of open concrete was not more than ten feet away.

"Get off, goddammit! You're killing my daughter!"

The weight atop them lessened further—enough that Riley began to crawl through the jungle of legs, pulling them across the rough surface on his elbows.

"Hang on," he said to Jenny, and she did.

Stangl

The girl on the guardroom radio stopped singing. Then came the sound of a gunshot. Stangl cocked his head. It had come from a small-caliber weapon without much killing power unless fired from close range. He smiled. Himmler had once claimed that hundreds of German spies and saboteurs were in America. If so, some must still be active and undoubtedly eager to continue the struggle despite the Führer's death. Perhaps one of them had killed the girl singer, despoiling the victory celebration in America.

...or ending the famous Farley Sackstead?

Stangl hadn't forgotten the insignificant pip-squeak who'd insulted him at a state dinner in Berlin, giving him his back rather than pay proper attention to a man whose stature warranted a seat just two chairs from the Führer. Stangl had vowed to avenge the slight and in the early days of the war believed the opportunity was imminent. By 1940 most of Europe had been overrun, and as the Battle of Britain raged in the skies over the United Kingdom, all of Germany expected that Nazi troops would soon march triumphantly through the streets of London. The American journalist's radio broadcasts originated there and Stangl had wangled an assignment with the provisional occupying force. Once installed he planned to hunt down the self-righteous little bastard and force him to watch as his Jew wife was executed. Afterward he would put the barrel of his Luger with its sleek silencer against Sackstead's skull, torturing the newsman with a few moments of terrifying anticipation before pulling the trigger.

"*Wir kämpfen für Deutschland! Wir kämpfen für Hitler!*"

Stangl reached down and touched his hip. He missed the feel of the Luger on his belt, its silencer poking through bottom of his holster and tapping on his thigh as he strode about Sobibor. The sound a bullet made when fired through a silencer was inexplicably stimulating for him, and, after hearing the characteristic *ptfft* for the first time in a crime film, he'd commissioned a gunsmith to make one for his standard-issue Luger. "This will produce significant kickback, Hauptsturmführer. Your aim will be disrupted," the man warned the officer, but Stangl hadn't cared until the incident with Private Zimmer in the barn. Afterward he'd removed the silencer and tucked it into the holster alongside the pistol, wanting his aim to be true should another Mauser be leveled on him.

Hudal had encouraged the SS officer to abandon the weapon before fleeing Europe. "If you're caught, this sort of sidearm will identify you as an officer. All officers will be detained for questioning, regardless of rank." Stangl knew the bishop was right but had kept the Luger anyway. It was a reminder of his rightful place in the world, the other trappings of rank and privilege taken from him: his stiff-necked uniform blouse, the high jackboots, the black officer's hat with an eagle on the peak and a skull-and-crossbones on the brim. Along with the sidearm they'd been as much a part of him as the priest's collar was to Hudal—emblems of merit and destiny, of faith and eminence.

The gun and silencer now belonged to the American major after Stangl's captors found it in a secret compartment of his suitcase. It would likely end up in a trophy case, he figured—attended by a lie of how it was obtained. Despite his own vanity Stangl was intolerant of conceit in others and disdained SS officers he'd known whose war mementos came with fictitious claims of peril and heroism even though the trophies were scrounged from corpses on spent battlefields or impounded from enlisted men powerless to protest. Kurth had been such a man. Stangl's aide had somehow garnered several campaign ribbons even though his involvement in the operations had been coincidental—perching on a chair outside the room where battle plans were discussed or delivering a message from his commanding officer to someone on the way to the front lines. Stangl wondered what had become of the vituperative little snake. Kurth had been last seen leaving their final posting in Vienna absent his uniform and the feathery toothbrush mustache he'd affected to curry favor with the Führer. Stangl chuckled.

A peacock stripped of his feathers.

Stangl didn't mourn the left-behind decorations that once decorated his own uniform. He'd never attached glory to trophies and medals. Metal tarnished with age, ribbons faded. Both would inevitably be forgotten relics in an attic shoebox.

But the world will not forget Franz Stangl!

The former commandant at Sobibor and Treblinka had presided over the deaths of more than a million, each name preserved in a set of leatherbound ledgers future historians would pore over, marveling at such monumental faithfulness and efficiency. They would write books about him, chronicle his place in the annals of time, preserve his life in print.

Ribbons are ephemeral. What is written is eternal.

Stangl heard approaching footsteps outside his cell and was unexpectedly visited by a memory: the defiant Wehrmacht colonel staring down the firing squad, his back ramrod straight, a cigarette in its holder jauntily clamped between his teeth. The man had been given the Führer's justice: swift, absolute, irrevocable. Promised a fair trial, he'd received only the sentence. The American major had promised Stangl a fair trial too, but the former SS officer understood that such promises were houses made of toothpicks—vows from conquerors not entirely in control of their conquering hordes. Such men preached honor and rules of war but were too distant from blood and death to understand irresistible impulse and the lust for bloody vengeance.

Besides…it is more expedient to shoot a prisoner than to guard one.

The footsteps grew louder and Stangl stood, using the flat of one hand to smooth his hair, afterward securing the top button on the shirt of his drab, prison-issue fatigues.

"Wir kämpfen für Deutschland! Wir kämpfen für Hitler!"

Eyes appeared in the view slit of his door and Stangl straightened, squaring his shoulders.

"Gut zielen," he whispered as a key was inserted into the doorlock. *Aim well.*

Jimmy

From across the Atlantic a muffled gunshot traversed the airwaves from Times Square in New York City to loudspeakers mounted on the fence enclosing Feucht Airfield. The sound took his breath away as it hurtled toward Jimmy like a German Messerschmitt with its cannons blazing. A prayer escaped his lips.

Not Jenny. Please God…not her.

The radio broadcast coming from the base loudspeakers was then filled with shouts rather than song, the voices building into a single wave of noise that made him forget about the snapped twigs echoing into the night and the flash of movement he'd seen at the edge of the woods. Head cocked, arm dangling at his side with Cap's .45 pointed at the ground, he prayed that the interruption of Jenny's performance had been nothing more than a forgotten lyric or a case of nerves, already grieving that she might have died before he could say goodbye—before he could tell her how much he loved her and how thankful he was to the little sister who had been forced to jump from girl to woman with the death of their mother.

The folks on Huron Street in Queens had praised him for being stalwart after Siobhan Doyle passed. "You're holding this family together," they'd told him, frowning at the slumped figure of his father on the porch of their tiny home, an empty bottle of Jameson at his feet. And Jimmy *had* stepped up, taking a weekend job on Coney Island where he ran the Loop-D-Loop ride and waiting tables at Sid's Diner in Queens four nights per week. Along with Mom's modest life insurance benefit, they'd gotten by, and the neighbors gave him most of the credit. But Jimmy knew it was Jenny who'd held them together. Four years younger than her brother, she'd dried her tears after Mom's funeral and gone to work, teaching herself to cook from their mother's recipe books, helping Dad stumble into bed after a bender, and refusing to let Jimmy quit school. "Don't even think about it!" she'd scolded him, her words and voice so channeling their mother it had made them both laugh. It was Jenny who'd kept house, darned their socks, made sure the bills were paid and the food never wasted; Jenny who'd put the brochures for City College on her brother's bed; Jenny who'd packed a lunch for him to eat on his way to basic training at Fort Benning; Jenny who'd cried alone in her room so the two men of the house would think she was okay.

From the distant loudspeakers Jimmy suddenly heard voices rise above the static of the faraway crowd in Times Square.

"Get the gun!"

"Get him!"

Simultaneously someone stepped into the open at the edge of the forest above him. Spectral and portentous—a silhouette in the dim moonlight—the figure rendered him momentarily powerless, so overwhelmed with regret he was unable to react. He didn't have to be here. He could have stayed home in America, gone to City College, maybe even Fordham. But he'd worked hard to graduate early from high school so he could enlist. Then he'd stupidly raised his hand when the wing commander asked for men with photography experience. Even dumber, he'd accepted his commanding officer's sidearm but disdained practice at the shooting range, left the base against Cap's advice, and now had strayed too far from the gates. Most of all, Jimmy Doyle bemoaned standing up in the knee-high grass on the shoulder of the road, giving the Nazi on the rise above him a better target. An instant later he shuddered away his regrets and was once again in the underside turret of the *Daisy Mae*, entering German air space with Cap's calm voice in his earpiece, the distant dots of Messerschmitts at six o'clock or nine o'clock or twelve o'clock or simply all the o'clocks.

We just don't give a damn anymore.

"Ich gebe auf," the figure above the road called out. "I give—"

Before the man could finish, a whistle pierced the night, a sound so like an artillery shell it made Jimmy grip Cap's .45 as if it were one of his fifties inside the Plexiglas bubble stuck to the belly of the *Daisy Mae*. He raised the gun, leveled it at the faceless figure, and fired. It was midnight, 0000 hours, on 8 May 1945 and Jimmy Doyle had fired the last shot of his war.

Gosia

"Fine," Rita, the midwife, grumped. "Have it your way. Try to push again." Gosia grasped the bedsheets as Rita once again positioned herself at the end of the bed. The contraction had arrived full force, the pain wrenching.

"Push," the midwife shouted.

Gosia pushed.

"Push harder!"

And Gosia did. She pushed harder, containing her scream. The girl on the radio had stopped singing, as if afraid her voice would distract mother and baby from their jobs.

"Wyjdz ze mnie!" Gosia shouted. *Get out of me!*

"Don't talk, dammit! Just push!" Rita scolded.

"Suka!" Aunt Ewa yelled. "Ty pieprzono suka!"

Gosia's first hours in America had been filled with shouting as well. They'd landed at on Long Island, where many of the soldiers on the transport had people waiting, relieved and teary-eyed family members calling out to husbands and sons and fathers. Farley Sackstead had arranged for a CBS car to meet her, and after she climbed into the rear seat the driver headed out, the city forming as they left Long Island, entered Queens, and then crossed the Queensboro Bridge into Manhattan. Gosia had been born and raised in Warsaw, but the suddenly bustling heart of New York City streets overwhelmed her. People yelled and cursed, cars honked, tires screeched. After the driver dropped her off at the building on East Fifty-Second Street where her aunt and uncle lived, she'd remained motionless in the parking lot that separated CBS headquarters from Jakub Dworak's Kosher Delicatessen, watching her uncle's stockboy wash the broad plate-glass window of the establishment. Eventually Aunt Ewa spotted her through the glass and rushed out.

"Oh, you poor thing...you poor, poor thing."

Gosia had quickly settled into her aunt and uncle's apartment above the deli—a two-bedroom affair combined with a studio where Ewa, an accomplished artist, had previously put paint to canvas. Gosia was given the studio, a bed and dresser replacing the easel and canvases. She'd immediately volunteered to work in the delicatessen.

"I want to be useful, Aunt Ewa."

"You'll be too much on your feet," the little woman cautioned, but Gosia insisted and was taught to run the cash register. The New Yorkers made her uncomfortable, talking too loudly, standing too close, thrusting opinions in all directions. Standoffish at first, they quickly accommodated to a new face behind the counter—the young men flirting, the old ones winking, the women determined to share their childbirth experiences even though Gosia understood nothing they said. The oddest was the Dworaks' landlord and neighbor—a wild-haired, pop-eyed woman who lived in the out-of-place, slumping house at the edge of the parking lot. "Here comes the Cat Woman... She's crazy," Aunt Ewa warned the first time Gosia saw Selma Filbert approach the store, stumbling along in her long winter overcoat and unbuckled galoshes. She'd entered the deli and then stopped at the counter long enough to look Gosia up and down before making for a door at the rear marked EMPLOYEES ONLY. Moments later she'd emerged with the stockboy, Riley. They left without saying goodbye, then crossed the parking lot and disappeared into the Cat Woman's lopsided house.

In a city filled with strange people, Gosia was quite certain the odd couple were the strangest—the old woman in the long wool coat worn on even the warmest of days and the thin, taciturn teenager with his thatch of black hair, pale complexion, and doleful demeanor. The Cat Woman was obviously insane, but the boy was an enigma—the typical silence he wore like a cloak rendering him forlorn and lost rather than ominous. He assiduously avoided eye contact with Gosia, although she'd occasionally caught him staring at her belly as if the life she carried inside could unravel the mystery of his own if he just looked long and hard enough.

The unmistakable sound of a gunshot echoed from Uncle Jakub's radio on the dresser, startling all three women. It was followed by a whistle and Gosia stopped pushing, shuddering at the same shrill, chilling sound the guards' whistles had made at Sobibor. The contraction began to fade. Simultaneously the door to the outer hallway was pushed open and the Cat Woman stepped into the small room. As always, she wore her winter overcoat and the buckles on her galoshes jangled. For a moment she stared at Rita, the midwife. Then the two women exchanged words suggestive of a past relationship that had ended badly. A moan involuntarily escaped Gosia's lips and the Cat Woman looked at her, at the same time retrieving a small vial of clear liquid from her coat pocket. She held it aloft like a scepter, speaking in English. Gosia looked to her aunt for help.

"Ona tu jest," Ewa paraphrased in translation. *She's here.*

Zimmer

The American on the road below remained motionless and Zimmer glanced at his watch. The minute hand had edged past twelve o'clock. If the timepiece was correct, the war was over and he could go home to Ingolstodt...to Ilse. Her last letter had reached him just before the end of mail delivery to the eastern front. The Wehrmacht troops were short of everything by then: ammunition, food rations, paper. He'd borrowed the nub of a pencil from Braun and written a reply on the back of her letter, closing with a promise. *Once I am home, we will never again be apart.* He'd meant it; yet he knew even then that his words were hollow. Ilse might be dead. God knew he'd nearly died trying to reach her, might yet die on this night if the American was too nervous or too scared or just too angry that Germany had ripped him from his home and thrust him into a nightmare of constant dread, occasional terror, and death.

More than once over the past five and half years Zimmer had welcomed the bullet that would grant him respite from the cold and hunger and fear. It was a perverse wish, one he'd also seen on the face of the man hiding in the grain silo. "Just empty your magazine into it!" Kurth had shouted from the ground that day. The fugitive inside the grain elevator had clearly known enough German to understand the words. He'd sighed and closed his eyes, his face sagging. Then he'd reopened them and looked up at Zimmer as if relieved. Their fates sealed, he and the woman—perhaps his wife—would not waste away in the death camp at Sobibor nor trudge the final steps to the chambers in Lager III. Death by gunfire would be mercifully quick and the man had turned the woman's face into his chest and then nodded at Zimmer. The moment had been oddly intimate.

Zimmer had disobeyed Kurth that day, refusing to empty his magazine into the silo as ordered. Instead, he'd waited until the rabid little weasel looked away, then glanced at the half-buried couple and put a finger to his lips before closing the top hatch and descending the ladder to the ground. Afterward he didn't share with anyone, even Braun, what he'd discovered on that late afternoon in November 1943, many times since wondering if the hidden fugitives had managed to avoid detection and survive. He hoped so. He'd risked a firing squad to spare them.

Zimmer squinted, trying to separate the details of the American's face from the night, to see if his expression reflected mercy or murder. But the man was too far away, the moonlight too pale, Zimmer's eyes too tired. Once again, the Wehrmacht soldier wondered if they were at a stalemate, no moves left for either of them. A moment later he smiled grimly. King Hitler—a madman who'd thrust millions of lives into harm's way to fulfill his pernicious and lustful ambition—had been checkmated. The game was over with nothing left to do but pick up the pawns like Zimmer and put them back in the pouch.

Zimmer took a deep breath and then called out as he stepped into the open.

"Ich gebe auf… I give—"

A gunshot interrupted him, followed by the same sound he'd heard just before Braun went down: the wet splat of a bullet striking flesh. The impact knocked him to the ground and filled him with a sense of imminence rather than pain. He looked up into the sky. Outside the shroud of forest he could see the full expanse of a firmament awash with stars. The luminescent specks were still bright—death not yet close enough to cloud his vision—and Zimmer was grateful. As he left the world the last things he'd see were the otherworldly constellations Herr Grohe had endeavored to teach him.

The girl on the radio had yet to resume her song. The young soldier was glad that neither the American national anthem nor Germany's would play him off the planet. Anthems and marches were not for soldiers in the field but for generals and politicians. The wars belonged to them. They claimed the glory, leaving regret and grief for others to bear. He closed his eyes, pictured Ilse, and waited for the dark of night to become the dark of forever.

This isn't so bad.

Then his leg began to throb and Zimmer winced, breathing a sigh of relief. The American may have shot to kill, but his aim had proven faulty. The wound was not fatal.

Riley

A body slammed into Riley as his gun discharged, the attendant report sounding more like an ember falling on water than a gunshot. The impact smashed him to the ground, the pistol knocked from his hand. He heard a whistle, a pop, shouts. The gun was just beyond his reach. Someone kicked it and a forest of feet and legs swallowed the weapon as people began to pile on, their weight pushing the air from his lungs and pressing him into the pavement.

It was happening again.

There had been six of them, none older than twelve. They were mean. He'd lost his job on the freighter. Pap had kicked him out and he'd returned to New York to find Jenny. The mean boys followed him after he left the train station, pushed him into an alley, put the point of a knife under his chin and another at his groin. They'd demanded money but were disappointed in their haul—four dollars and his army jacket—afterward throwing him against the brick wall. He'd fallen and they'd kicked and beaten him with their fists, calling him names and laughing.

"*Retard… Imbecile!*"

Curled into a ball, his face pressed against concrete fragrant with spent Juicy Fruit gum, leaked engine oil, and urine, Riley had waited for the end, hoping his mother wasn't as mean in Heaven as she'd been on Earth.

"*Imbecile…fucking imbecile!*"

The Cat Woman had saved him. Materializing in the mouth of the alley, she'd pulled Carl's pistol from the pocket of her long overcoat and fired a single shot into the air. Momentarily startled, the mean boys had then laughed and fearlessly charged her, skidding to a stop when the next two bullets ricocheted off the cement at their feet. A fourth shot had sent them running.

Afterward the Cat Woman approached Riley, standing over him and studying his face with its oddly curled upper lip.

"Where's your tail?" she'd asked.

"Ain't got one."

"All cats have tails. Where's yours?"

"I told you... Ain't got one."

She'd turned and walked away without another word, Riley trailing her from the alley and then down West Thirty-Fourth Street. Despite her age and a limp, her pace had been brisk and he'd nearly lost her when he paused to stare up at the towering Empire State Building, tipping his head so far back he'd nearly fallen over. Only her wild tangle of hair was visible when he lowered his eyes back to the street and chased after her, catching up as she turned onto Fifth Avenue. She'd led him past Bryant Park with its leafy canopy of trees in the midst of brick and mortar; through the Diamond District filled with heavily bearded men, their side curls spilling out from beneath funny hats; and past the ice rink in Rockefeller Plaza, its golden Prometheus statue awaiting winter and the skaters who would glide about under the Maker of Mortal's watchful eye. When they reached the parking lot for the CBS building, she'd stopped long enough to point at the HELP WANTED sign in the window of Jakub Dworak's Kosher Delicatessen, then continued on to the crumbling home perched on one corner of the lot.

Unable to breathe, Riley fought to get up as more weight piled on and confetti trickled through the melee, settling like giant red, white, and blue snowflakes.

"Light as a feather, buddy..."

At boot camp they'd made the men each carry a comrade across an obstacle course while the sergeant fired bullets at their heels—practice if called upon to save someone felled on the field of battle. Riley and Jimmy had buddied up and Jimmy easily toted his slender friend across the course. "You can do it, Riley," he'd encouraged him. "I'm light as a feather, buddy... Light as a feather!" And Riley *had* done it, summoning strength that surprised him as he stumbled through the drill with Jenny's brother on his shoulders. His time was slower than Jimmy's but not the slowest in the platoon.

"*You can do it, Riley!*"

Summoning all his strength, Riley managed to wriggle onto his back, his face close to the person who'd knocked him to the ground.

Jenny!

She was frightened, her eyes wide. He tried to speak, but no sound came out.

I love you.

Riley worked his arms free, then reached over Jenny's shoulders and put his hands on the chest of a man atop her. Gathering his strength, he pushed until enough weight had been lifted for them both to breathe.

"*Light as a feather, buddy… Light as a feather!*"

"I love you," he told Jenny, exhaling as his strength gave out and air once again leaked from his lungs under the ponderous mass of bodies. Then he heard her father's voice.

"You're crushing my daughter!"

The weight began to lessen, allowing Riley and Jenny to breathe as bodies atop them were pulled off. She lifted her head, her eyes coming into better focus.

"*She's the nicest person you'll ever know.*"

"I love you," he told her.

He rolled onto his belly. An open patch of concrete was just a few feet away and Riley began to crawl toward it with Jenny hanging on, the Cat Woman's words ringing in his ears.

"*That girl will love you.*"

Antoni

After Antoni and Janusz retrieved Gosia from the forest, Tillie had allowed the escapees a night's sleep before assigning them chores. "Work will help," she told them. "Staying busy comforts the mind." Janusz had been skeptical, eyeing Antoni's thin physique. "No muscle for work," he'd sniffed. "Won't be much help from the looks of him." But the big farmer had underestimated his new hand. Hard labor and extra scraps of food Gosia snuck to her husband from the commandant's stores had made the former translator at Sobibor lean and sinewy, and he kept up with Janusz as they prepared the farm for winter. "Not too bad for a Warsaw city boy," the big farmer conceded at the end of the first week. Meanwhile, Tillie kept Gosia busy in the house, where the girls were quickly charmed by their beautiful houseguest, following her about like imprinted ducklings. Evenings, they spent in the parlor where Antoni told stories drawn from *The Arabian Nights* and Gosia played an upright piano, her finger memory quickly returning after just a night or two. November arrived and they all began to relax—Tillie and the girls thinking of the fugitives as family, Janusz becoming less grumpy, Antoni and Gosia miraculously believing they might actually be safe.

Then the Germans came.

"They're in the forest!" Krystyna, the eldest daughter, breathlessly cried out after bursting from the woods surrounding the farm. Antoni was in the field that day, helping Janusz use the tiller to chop flattened yellow cornstalks into mulch while Gosia sliced beets in the kitchen. The fugitive couple met at the silo, then scrambled up the outside, lifted the hatch, and cautiously descended the interior ladder until waist-deep in seed corn. They heard the Germans sweep onto the property and Untersturmführer Kurth—the junior officer Stangl had assigned to lead the search detail—barking orders at his men in German, the officer's voice easily heard through the silo wall.

"Shoot anyone you find! We need to get back before dark! The damned Russians are everywhere."

Gosia had looked to her husband to translate.

"He's worried about Russians," he whispered. "Wants them to hurry."

"That's all he said?"

"Yes."

With Kurth shouting at his men to go faster the Germans had scoured the farmstead, the SS officer's voice competing with the clucking chickens and bleating goats wandering about the property. Eventually, with his eyes on the eastern horizon, he'd preempted further inspection.

"There's no one here. Let's go!"

Inside the silo, choking dust was suspended in thin slices of sunlight slanting between the planks of the top hatch. It made their eyes water and their noses run. Gosia sneezed and moments later the silo began to quiver as heavy boots shook the rungs of the ladder clinging to the outside of the tower. "Duck under if someone looks in from the top," Janusz had advised when planning for the moment now upon them. "But don't let go of the ladder. You'll sink to the bottom and smother. It's like dry quicksand in there." Antoni and Gosia had taken deep breaths and lowered themselves beneath the surface of the loose seed corn. They'd next heard the hatch open, felt the warmth of the sun flood into the silo and through the ocean of corn, heard Kurth call out again.

"Leeren sie einfach ihr magazin hinein!" *Just empty your magazine into it!*

Ten seconds elapsed, then twenty…then thirty. As one minute approached Gosia could no longer hold her breath. She'd pulled free and climbed the ladder until her head was above the seed corn. Antoni followed, emerging from the rolling surface to see a poster-worthy, square-jawed Aryan peering down at them through the open hatch. "I love you," he'd whispered to Gosia, turning her face away from the eye of the gun barrel as they waited for the final explosion of bullets that would end their lives. But the soldier never fired his weapon, instead putting a finger on his lips to silence them, afterward calling out to Kurth.

"Alles clar, Herr Untersturmführer… Nichts hier." *All clear… Nothing here.*

The view slit in the otherwise solid metal door of Stangl's cell was dark, the light inside turned off. Antoni leaned forward to look through the opening. Ramrod straight, Franz Stangl stood as if at attention in the middle of the small room. Faintly illuminated by light from the corridor, he suddenly recognized the eyes in the view slit and his lips curled into the hint of a sneer. It was a final insult that erased Antoni's memories of the farm and the silo and the young German soldier, replacing them with the violent image of Stangl atop Gosia, thrusting himself in and out of her.

Have you ever had such a man as I?

Antoni's fingers tightened around the grip of the Luger and he inserted the key into the lock. At the same time, Stangl's sneer dissolved into a serpentine smile and the former commandant of the death camp at Sobibor straightened even more, defiantly thrusting his jaw forward as if defiance, alone, could save him.

7

8 May 1945

1800:00 to 1815:00 Eastern Standard Time
0000:00 to 0015:00 Central European Time

Farley

Blood dribbled from the wound in Nobbie Wainwright's forehead as he sat up, the butt end of a 0.22 slug visible in the hole. The former sportscaster touched the wound, stared at his bloody fingers, and then passed out, his head producing a thud when it hit the wood planks that formed the floor of the booth. On the street outside the broadcast booth, people pushed, shoved, and punched each other as they tried to run for safety, the melee made curiously noiseless by the thick glass. Suddenly their yelling and cursing poured into the enclosure when the door was pushed open and a soldier in uniform rushed in. He knelt beside Nobbie, held fingers against his neck, and then bent to put his ear next to the stricken man's mouth.

"Pulse is fine. He's breathing."

The soldier, a naval medical corpsman, gently probed the skin around Nobbie's wound and then plucked the 0.22 slug from it.

"Borrow a pen?" he asked Farley. The journalist handed one to him and the corpsman extracted Nobbie's pocket square, then placed it over the wound and used the cap end of the pen to dab at it. Afterward he reinspected the wound. "It's not deep," he said to Farley. "Bullet never fully penetrated the skull."

"He's pretty hardheaded," Farley replied.

"Nobody's *that* hardheaded. Cartridge must have been defective…damp gunpowder or something."

A knock on the glass separating the broadcast cubicles drew Farley's attention. He looked to the sound. The engineer had come out from under his desk. His headphones were back in place, his lips moving.

You're on the air. Keep going!

"He'll be all right?" Farley asked the corpsman.

The naval medic nodded. "He'll have a hell of a headache, but yeah...he'll be all right."

Farley picked up his microphone and looked out through the glass. The stage—now covered in red, white, and blue confetti—was otherwise empty, the various dignitaries who'd been in a lather to get attention before the gunshot considerably less sanguine about their prospects after it. On the street below the stage, the shooter and young Jenny Doyle had disappeared, hidden beneath a growing mound of people.

"You've just heard the sounds of an attack on this reporter, ladies and gentlemen," Farley began. "An unidentified young man burst from the crowd and fired a shot at me. It missed, instead wounding producer Nobbie Wainwright who is presently being attended by a returning member of our Armed Forces. I'm told the wound is superficial and Nobbie will be all right. However..."

Farley hesitated. Outside the booth the singer had reappeared. "Ladies and gentlemen," he intoned, speaking quietly as she regained the stage and moved toward the microphones at the center. "Young Jenny Doyle...the fifteen-year-old girl from Queens, New York, who heroically helped subdue the gunman...has returned to the stage. She—"

He didn't finish, his throat suddenly full as the girl began to sing, her voice strong and brave.

"'O'er the land...'"

Farley felt tears forming, his throat knotted. He'd listened to countless singers render equally countless versions of "The Star-Spangled Banner." Beyond childhood the hymn had never stirred him because the America he'd known was less a land of freedom and bravery than one of avarice and acquisition.

Growing up in an Indiana factory town, the son of union organizer Owen Sackstead, he'd witnessed racism and union busting. Later covering stories around the world for the *Tribune* he'd seen the effects of American dollar diplomacy—tyrants and tyrannic regimes supported in exchange for a benevolent attitude toward U.S. commerce. But now, as Jenny Doyle sang to a crowd again growing quiet, he finally understood what had moved Francis Scott Key in 1814 when he saw the American flag still waving over Fort McHenry after twenty-five hours of bombardment by British artillery. For nearly six long years victors and vanquished alike had suffered the rockets' red glare, the bombs bursting in air—millions of unseen and unknown faces across the globe, along with the hundreds of unforgettable ones Farley had encountered during the perilous fight and the decade that preceded it. Among them were an ominous, toothbrush-mustachioed chancellor of Germany; his arrogant SS sycophant; a teenaged combat veteran who dreamed of an unguaranteed future from his belly gunner's turret; a miraculous couple now poised to bring life into the world in defiance of those who had taken the lives of millions like them; and last of all, a courageous fifteen-year-old girl who'd risked her life for a man she knew only from his voice on the radio.

Why had she done it?

Perhaps it was reactive, Farley pondered. Perhaps vainglorious. And then he knew. Listening to her beautiful voice fill Times Square and move so many in the assembled throng to tears, he remembered being young and believing in things. His years abroad and the war had rubbed the luster off his American dream. But he'd once been a believer too. A long time ago he'd been like Jenny Doyle and her soldier brother, ready to risk his life because America could be a land of the free only if it were truly the home of the brave.

Nobbie Wainwright, while dazed, had regained consciousness and, with the naval corpsman's help, managed to sit up. Farley glanced at him, then again spoke into his microphone, his eyes on Jenny Doyle.

"Ladies and gentlemen here in America and across the world..." he began. His voice cracked and he hesitated, trying to collect himself. For a few moments on this jubilant evening in New York City he'd peered at the end of his life. It was a story that might earn a headline in tomorrow morning's paper. But he knew it wasn't the only story. As this war wound down and another still raged on the other side of the globe, there were millions of stories.

Farley set his microphone on the desk and listened as the young fifteen-year-old girl from Queens finished the song, her face open and uplifted, her voice resounding and unbroken. Her story would not end on this night, and for her sake, Farley vowed to ensure it would be lived by telling a different story—the one that had hurtled humanity into this moment. It would be a cautionary tale, warning the world not to forget its past, and he hoped it would be enough.

Selma

"I flunked you," Selma growled at the midwife, Rita. "You shouldn't be here."

Rita's expression wrinkled into a pout. "I took the course again. With a different instructor. You weren't the only one, you know."

"Which instructor...Kaiser? Or Larsen?"

"Larsen."

"Figures."

Selma flung an arm outward as if to dismiss her former student.

"Now move," she added.

Rita didn't budge. "She needs a doctor, Mrs. Filbert. She's OC...and narrow ischial spines. I don't—"

"Move, Rita."

"I think she needs a C-section—"

"I said move," Selma hissed.

Rita bared her teeth like a terrier, looking as if she might bark. Then she rolled her lips inward and swallowed her anger.

"Fine," she said, shrugging as she stepped away. "Knock yourself out. See if you can get anywhere with this one. I sure haven't."

Selma took Rita's place at the end of the bed. "We need to let gravity to help us," she told the girl's aunt. "Squatting will widen the pelvis…make more room. She… What's her name?"

"Gosia," Mrs. Dworak told her.

"Okay… Gosia has to get out of bed. Tell her that."

The aunt translated the instructions and they helped the laboring mother climb out of bed and then assume a squat on the floor next to it. Rita watched.

"Looks like you've got this—" she began.

"Get out," Selma barked.

Rita recoiled as if slapped, then glowered at her former instructor.

"Gladly," she bit back. "More power to you."

With the midwife's footsteps echoing on the hardwood stairs outside the apartment, Selma took pillows from the bed and placed them on the floor beneath the laboring mother. Afterward she smiled at her.

"I'm going to put my hand on your tummy, okay, Gosia? I won't hurt you… I promise."

The aunt translated and Gosia nodded. Then Selma rested a hand on the young woman's abdomen, head tipped as if listening for the sound of the next contraction.

"Time to push again," she said, looking at the girl's aunt. "She must then push without making a sound. Tell her that, okay?"

Ewa did and the young woman closed her eyes, took a deep breath, and bore down.

Selma dropped to her knees and put her hands beneath Gosia's bedgown. "How do you say, 'Push'?" she asked Ewa.

"Naciskać,"

"Okay…naciskać, Gosia," Selma said. "Keep naciskaćing!"

Gosia pushed and pushed, then released her breath in a howl, sucked in a huge gulp of air and pushed again.

"That's it," Selma encouraged, her hands still beneath Gosia's gown. "I can feel the head. The baby's coming. One more push, dear. One more naciskać."

"Naciskać, Gosia!" Ewa urged. "Nasciskać!"

"Naciskać, Gosia!"

The young Polish woman continued to push, her face turning dusky, the veins on her forehead pronounced.

"Stop pushing!" Selma shouted. The infant's head was out, the umbilical cord wrapped around its neck. The aunt translated, Gosia rested, and Selma then carefully pulled the cord over the baby's head.

"Little naciskać," she said, without looking up.

"Moly nasick," the girl's aunt told her niece, watching with tears in her eyes as her crazy neighbor and landlord—Selma Filbert, the Cat Woman—carefully delivered the rest of the infant, afterward bringing him out from under his mother's gown as an exhausted Gosia collapsed onto the pillows they'd placed on the floor.

The room was now quiet save the sounds of crowd noise coming from the radio. The baby was silent, too, its face blue. Selma held the newborn against her bosom for warmth, murmuring as she gently wiggled his chin with her finger until he began to cry. Meanwhile, the aunt helped Gosia climb back into bed. Afterward Selma wrapped the child in a blanket and then handed him to his mother.

"How do you say 'boy'?" she asked Mrs. Dworak.

"Chłopak."

Selma smiled at Gosia. "It's a chłopak," she said. "Have you picked a name?"

Gosia understood the question without her aunt's help.

"Józef," she said. "Józef Farley Pietkowski."

"Farley?"

"A promise," Gosia explained. "If boy, is Farley. Mister Sackstead say, 'No, he American...name Joe.'" She smiled. "So...name both."

Selma looked around the room, then up at the ceiling. She

remembered it all: this studio apartment and Father, the faint sensation of life inside her own womb. Later came the fever and aches, the lumps on her neck, the little white footprints in her brain only the mysterious X-rays could see. It had killed her only child, this disease the Carolines and the Rogers and the Sidneys had given her. Some survivors had trouble with their vision, she'd read in her textbooks. Some began to see and hear things that weren't there. "Most recover," the doctors had promised, but some didn't and Selma hadn't.

The darkness, heavy and smothering, had once again begun to settle over her and Selma took a vial of Miracle Holy Water from her overcoat, poured its contents into her hand, and then gently rubbed the water onto the baby's open fontanelle.

"Welcome to America, Józef," she said as the girl on the radio returned and began once again to sing the national anthem, her voice as pure and innocent and filled with promise as Józef Farley Pietkowski. Selma watched the newborn infant attempt to suckle at his mother's breast. Then she put the remaining vials of Miracle Holy Water on the bedside table.

"You're going to need these," she said as a puzzled expression formed on the young woman's face. "Farley is a bad name."

Jenny

Confetti drifted down from the buildings bordering Times Square as Riley crawled free of the melee, pulling himself along on his elbows. Jenny clung to him, arms wrapped around his neck. The crowd thinned as they neared the steps leading to the glass-walled booth, enough that Jenny could climb off Riley's back. They stood, facing each other, and she took both his hands in hers. A voice called out, rising above the crowd.

"Jenny!"

She looked to the sound. Thirty feet and a jumble of revelers and amateur pugilists away, her father fought to reach her. The two lamppost cops were close behind, poking people with their nightsticks, a few of the drunker men in uniform winding up to throw punches that wilted in the face of badges and hard-set cop jaws. Most of the fighting had stopped. Instead, strangers hugged and kissed and children were lifted onto their fathers' shoulders, their tiny hands trying to catch the red, white, and blue streamers. The wars in Times Square and Europe were both over.

"Get away from him, Jenny!" Dad yelled.

Jenny kept her eyes locked on Riley's, their fingers linked together. Rising up on tiptoes, she put her face next to his and whispered in his ear. And then he was gone, disappearing into the crowd as if absorbed by it. Moments later her father and the two policemen reached her.

"Where did he go?" one of the cops demanded. He was the younger of the pair, a thick rasp of black chest hair spilling over his open shirt collar, a shadow of beard on his face.

She shook her head. "I don't know… I have to finish." She took a step toward the steps leading to the stage. The young cop stopped her with a hand on her arm.

"Now, just hold on—"

"I have to finish," Jenny repeated, leveling blue eyes on him.

The older cop had hair tinged with gray, his belly gently fighting his service belt. "Seems like you knew him, miss," he said to Jenny. "The shooter."

She shook her head. "I didn't."

The older cop nodded, studying Jenny and then her father.

"What about you?" he asked Brian Doyle.

"He doesn't know him either," Jenny said.

"I was asking your father, miss."

"I already told you," Jenny said. "We don't know him… either of us, right, Dad?"

"Jenny—" Brian Doyle began.

"We don't know him," Jenny repeated, eyeing her father. "Now please get out of the way, officers. I have to finish." The younger cop was unmoved, his hand remaining on her arm. Jenny appraised the older one. He was fair-skinned and clean shaven, his badge shiny, his nameplate identifying him as O'Neill. "You're Irish," Jenny said. "Me too. I'm Jenny Doyle."

O'Neill studied Jenny for a moment, lips pursed. Then he nodded. "It's okay, Dom," he said. "Let her go. We've got her name. The detectives can follow up."

The younger cop released her arm and Jenny made her way back to the stage, looking through the glass of the broadcast booth as she climbed the steps. The man who'd been shot lay on the floor, a soldier in uniform at his side. The famous journalist, Farley Sackstead, was standing—his grenade-shaped desk microphone in his hand, his lips moving. Jenny reached the stage and began to cross it. The platform was now empty of people—Mayor LaGuardia and the other dignitaries evacuated by their security details, the snotty PA and the rest of the stage-management team running for their lives after the gun appeared. Jenny reached the cluster of microphones at center stage and looked out over the throng. The scattered fights had devolved into hurled insults, a few soldiers rubbing their cheeks after uninvited kisses earned well-deserved slaps. Half the faces were pointed at her and slowly the other half joined them.

"'O'er the land,'" she began, then stopped—relief and gratitude putting a lump in her throat. Jimmy was alive, his war over, and she'd helped his sad friend escape, just as her brother would have wanted. She could focus again, making certain she did not forget the lyrics to the anthem or lose her pitch in the reverberation of the speakers or freeze in the face of an audience numbering in the thousands. The end was in sight if she could just send the last few words and notes of the national anthem into the evening air.

The crowd had turned eerily quiet, their faces filled with uncertainty as they waited for Jenny to resume, the war perhaps not truly over for them until the last note of "The Star-Spangled Banner" had trailed off. Their attentiveness helped her settle, her tears retreating, her throat relaxing until she was no longer nervous or worried about the length of her performance. She was off the clock and could now finish the national anthem however she liked—surging to an unscored high note, pausing dramatically, and then closing with an assured run to celebrate the moment as it should be celebrated.

"'O'er the land of the free,'" she reprised, the crowd now hers, the lyrics of their national anthem a reminder that the job was not over. On the other side of the planet, more rockets revealed their red glare, more bombs burst in air as a different war raged on. It was now nearly fifteen minutes after midnight in Europe where devastation had been replaced, for now, with peace. It wasn't everything, Jenny realized, but it would have to be enough as she went on, singing to New York City, America, and the world at large, her words clear and sincere and hopeful.

Stangl

The overhead light bulb came on, the door opened, and Antoni Pietkowski stepped into the cell. Stangl's Luger was in his hand, the custom-made silencer attached. Stangl had once bragged that his resolve would not flag if fate stood him before a firing squad. But now the boast was about to be redeemed and his tenacity flagged as he imagined with dread the spit of the Luger. There would be no escape. The bullet would pierce his heart, the world would fade and turn black, and he would then realize the once unimaginable notion that Hauptsturmführer Franz Stangl—the imperial commandant at Sobibor and Treblinka, the favorite of Himmler and Hitler, and the man once feared as the White Death—no longer existed.

Stangl backed up until he thudded into the unrelenting cinderblock wall.

"Bitte...ich habe befehle befolgt," he whimpered. *Please...I was following orders.*

Antoni's face darkened. "Jetze sind sie an der reihe, sich zu entschuldigen," he said. *It's your turn to apologize.*

"Was?" *What?*

"Sich entschuldigen." *Apologize.*

Stangl began to babble in German, attempting to beg for his life without the humiliation of actual begging. "Your wife... She is fine, yes? How is your wife, your Gosia? Of course, I was very relieved when I learned you were both alive. *Very* relieved. We ended things…badly, I fear. Unfortunate, but times as they were. Circumstances… She is with you here in Austria, yes? Please tell her hello from me. Yes, tell her hello from Franz—"

"Apologize and I'll finish it quickly," Antoni interrupted, speaking in German.

"Yes, give her my very best… And be sure to tell her how happy I am that you both escaped. *So* happy. A terrible place… the camp. You realize, of course, that we were all victims in a way. I was forced to obey orders. I did not want to, but I had no choice, did I? Hitler did not give us choices, did he? No, he did not. But I never thought it would come to…I never wanted—"

He was interrupted again, this time by the journalist, Farley Sackstead, the instantly recognizable voice coursing down the cellblock from the radio in the guardroom, his words as foreign to Stangl as the otherworldly buzz in his ears.

"You've just heard the sounds of an attack on this reporter, ladies and gentlemen…"

Sackstead went on until the girl singer intervened, reclaiming the airwaves in a voice stronger and more resolved.

"'O'er the land…'"

Antoni's lips parted slightly and he lifted his eyes, looking past Stangl as if he could see an image of the faraway singer on the cinderblock wall.

"She is a very good singer, the American woman, yes?" Stangl gibbered in German. "Perhaps you will go to America now too?"

Antoni lowered his gaze, head cocked as if puzzled.

"God bless America," Stangl nattered, his head bobbing up and down. "And God bless Roosevelt too… No, God Bless Truman now, yes? God bless Harry Tru—"

"Was it a translator you wanted," Antoni cut him off. "Or a witness?"

"What?"

"That was it, wasn't it? My life spared…for a time, anyway… to preserve your legacy?"

It was the glimmer of a reprieve and Stangl began to nod feverishly in agreement, the pitch of his voice rising as his words spilled out faster and faster.

"Yes, that was it... I needed a witness. Of course you saw that, Antoni. You were always so insightful, so intelligent...the *most* intelligent of all those at Sobibor. Of course, that is why I spared you. You must not forget that. I *spared* you. And I spared *Gosia*."

"Stop talking," Antoni said.

He cocked the hammer of the Luger, the sound echoing throughout the tiny cell. Stangl fell to his knees, bowing his head, his hands covering his face.

"Bitte...bitte," he sobbed.

The Luger answered him. Once, twice, three times it spat. Then silence, save the broadcast emanating from the guardroom radio. The American national anthem had ended, a different singer taking over. Stangl recognized the voice: the Black American woman, Billie Holiday. The song was "God Bless the Child," a piece Stangl had once enjoyed before Hitler declared it a pagan spiritual.

Now it is my funeral dirge.

Miss Holiday sang several lines of the song before Stangl could summon the courage to tentatively spread his fingers and peek between them. The air was filled with feathers. Antoni had retreated and was framed in the doorway. "Auf wiedersehen, Hauptsturmführer," he said. The former interpreter at Sobibor stepped into the corridor and the heavy door swung shut. The view slit was then shuttered and the single overhead light bulb inside the cell extinguished. Stangl crumpled to the floor, the cramped chamber deprived of light suddenly more spare, the foul smells—mildew, sweat, urine—more pervasive.

Curled up like an infant, the once-proud SS officer wept sloppily, his tears and snot pooling on the cold stony floor, his once proud Aryan chin quivering with relief and sorrow and regret. He was alone—stripped of anger and arrogance, of destiny and dignity, of comfort and companionship. He opened his eyes, struggling to make out shapes in the utter darkness. There were none. Instead, he visualized a reckoning, a future as inescapable as the damp, dismal cell that now caged him. Piercing with sunken eyes and pointing with bony fingers, they would testify. They would accuse. They would tell the truth, revealing that he'd not followed orders to be dutiful, but because he reveled in it. They had been nothing to him but numbers called from a list. Now, in a moment of uncharacteristic prescience and self-awareness, Hauptsturmführer Franz Stangl—the man they'd called the White Death—understood that a day loomed ahead when his own number would at last be called as well.

Jimmy

Jimmy once again dove into the roadside grass, landing on his belly and then curling into a ball as he waited for return gunfire. Instead, from near the tree line above the road, he heard a low moan followed by a few words.

"Ich gebe auf… Ich gebe auf, du idiota!"

"Speak English. I don't understand Kraut!"

"I…give up. Ich gebe auf. I give up."

Jimmy cautiously lifted his head, then rose to a crouch, Cap's .45 pointed at the voice.

"C'mon outta there. And speak English. No spreche sie Deutsch, get it?"

"Du hast auf mich geschossen…gott verdammt!" *You shot me, goddammit!*

Jimmy understood *gott verdammt* and laughed. "Goddammit is right, Fritz," he murmured. He lowered himself back into the cover of the high grass. He'd heard stories of Germans who'd supposedly surrendered only to produce a hidden weapon. He needed to be patient. The gunshot had likely been heard at the base. Someone would be sent to investigate.

"Don't get cute, Fritz," he yelled. "Somebody's gonna be here any minute. Just hang tight and we'll both be okay."

"Ich spreche kein Englisch, Joe." *I don't speak English.*

Jimmy rolled onto his back and looked up into the night sky. It was clear, the constellations bright, their star clusters easily identifiable. *Orion's belt, the Big Dipper, the Little Dipper.*

Nearly a minute passed without the sound of approaching voices or the growl of a Jeep engine.

"Got us a Mexican standoff, don't we, Fritz?" Jimmy called out.

The German above the road remained silent for a moment, then shouted back.

"Mexikaner?"

"Yeah...Mexican. You know...Zorro, Cisco Kid."

More silence followed, then, "Ja, *La Marca de Zorro*...Tyrone Power."

Jimmy smiled. The Kraut was a movie fan. Jimmy was too. He'd taken Maeve to see Tyrone Power in *The Mark of Zorro* on their first date. Maeve's mother had insisted on a chaperone, reluctantly granting permission after Jimmy offered to bring Jenny along. "I'm going to marry Zorro and you can marry Maeve," his ten-year-old sister announced as the credits scrolled down the screen. "We'll live next door to each other."

Jimmy wondered what Maeve was doing. Was she in Times Square? Was she with someone? They'd met in high school. She was pretty with sandy hair and green eyes. He was smart and funny and a track star. They'd seemed perfect together and everyone assumed they'd fall in love, even though neither felt love so much as obligation. Maeve envisioned marriage, children, a husband who turned over his paycheck, and a house within walking distance of her mother, while Jimmy knew that Maeve was what Siobhan Doyle would have wanted for her son: an Irish girl anxious to make grandchildren. He closed his eyes, trying to visualize Maeve's face. They'd met in a Spanish class at John Adams High.

Spanish class...La Marca de Zorro... He speaks Spanish!

Jimmy rolled over, then rose to a crouch, his head above the high grass, gun pointed.

"Hey, Fritz," he called out. "Manos arriba."

From thirty feet away two hands appeared above the knee-high brush and Jimmy cautiously regained his feet, then scaled the embankment and negotiated the gentle rise to the edge of the woods. He found the German in a patch of flattened grass. The wounded man had placed a tourniquet around one leg, using the strap from his rucksack. He was pissed off.

"I was giving up and you shot me, you idiot!" he growled in Spanish.

"Estas armado?" Jimmy demanded. *Are you armed?*

The German shook his head and Jimmy motioned with the gun. "No funny business, got it?" he said. "You try something, I'll put one between your eyes."

"Tódavia no hablo Ingles, Joe." *Still don't speak English.*

"Manos abajo, esta bien?" Jimmy replied. *Hands down, okay?*

The German lowered his arms and Jimmy holstered his gun, then knelt to examine the wound. The Wehrmacht soldier had been hit in the fleshy part of his upper leg, an exit wound on the back side.

"You're lucky," Jimmy said in Spanish. "It's through and through."

The German snorted. "I'm not lucky. You're a lousy shot."

Jimmy scowled, then spoke in English. "Put me behind my fifties, I'd shoot your goddamned head off, Fritz."

"Que?" *What?*

"Nada…no es importante."

Jimmy pulled the tourniquet tighter, then helped the wounded soldier to his feet. Afterward he half-carried him down the slope to the road as Jenny's voice once again began to resound from the base loudspeakers. He breathed a sigh of relief.

"That's my little sister on the radio, Fritz," he said in English.

"En Espanol, Joe."

Jimmy repeated the words in Spanish and the German nodded with approval.

"Buena cantante," he said. *Good singer.*

The German's Spanish was very good, Jimmy's good enough

for them to carry on a rudimentary conversation as they made their way toward the airfield. It was now several minutes after midnight and Billie Holiday's voice was on the radio, singing "God Bless the Child." They breached the sharp curve in the roadway and the base loomed head, high-powered lamps mounted on the gates bathing them in light. Two men emerged as they neared the guardhouse, their rifles at the ready. "Who goes there?" one called out. A moment later the sentry recognized the *Daisy Mae*'s belly gunner and lowered his weapon.

"Whatcha got there, Jimmy?"

"Picked me up a stray, Stan."

The guard handed over his weapon to the other soldier, then helped Jimmy support the wounded German as they moved toward the airfield with Billie Holiday providing accompaniment.

"I like this one," the German said in Spanish as they passed through the gates.

"What did he say?" Stan asked.

"He likes this song," Jimmy told him.

"Tell 'im I like it too," Stan said.

They turned onto a narrow pathway and saw the base infirmary.

"Hey, Fritz," Jimmy posed. "Como se llama?" *What's your name?*

"Eckhardt," the German told him. "Eckhardt Zimmer."

"Me llamo Jimmy…Jimmy Doyle."

"Ich gebe auf, Jimmy Doyle," the German said. "I give up."

Jimmy laughed.

"Yeah…I know, Eckhardt," he replied as they continued toward the infirmary, a single light over its entrance glowing like a guide star.

Gosia

"Mrs. Filbert wants you to squat beside the bed…make more room for the baby," Ewa told her niece in Polish.

Gosia shook her head.

"No. Take me to a hospital. I want a doctor."

"Gosia—"

"No! She's crazy, Aunt Ewa. I want a real doctor!"

Ewa and the Cat Woman carried on an exchange in English. Then Gosia's aunt spoke to her niece.

"It's too late. It'll be fine. Mrs. Filbert is a midwife too. She trained Rita."

Gosia felt faint tension in her abdomen as another contraction began. She sighed. Her aunt was right. It was too late.

"Dobra," she said. *Okay.*

With help, Gosia climbed out of bed and assumed a squat on the hardwood floor. The Cat Woman put a hand on her belly. "Time to push again," she said.

Aunt Ewa translated and then Gosia took a deep breath, ground her eyes shut, and pushed, bearing down with all her strength for what seemed an impossibly long time. About to pass out, she released her breath in a violent rush, sucked in more air and pushed again, the room ominously darkening as her baby stubbornly maintained his purchase inside her womb. How long had it been? How long would it take? How much more did she have left? Suddenly Gosia wanted to die and be done with it—to leave this accursed mortal body with an elephant stuck in its pelvis. She was exhausted, frantic, frustrated, angry, desperate, despondent, despairing. Then she somehow found a way to carry on and pushed harder.

"Naciskać, Gosia... Nasciskac!"

"Zamknać się!" she screamed. *Shut up!*

She took another deep breath and bore down again, lips curled inward to contain her scream. The Cat Woman was on her knees, her hands under Gosia's bedgown, head bent to reveal a small patch of nearly bald scalp.

"Stop!" she abruptly called out, holding up a hand.

"Nie naciskać!" Ewa shouted. *Don't push!*

Gosia felt the Cat Woman's hands doing something with the baby. Then the old woman looked up.

"Little push," she said.

Ewa translated and Gosia pushed. Only a little. The tiniest push. One that hardly seemed enough until miraculously it was, the pressure in her pelvis abating and then gone. Gosia fell back onto the pillows, her baby forgotten as she stared at a crack in the ceiling plaster. The room had gone mercifully quiet, save crowd noise coming from the radio.

"C'mon now," the Cat Woman murmured softly.

Gosia propped herself up on her elbows. Her baby had yet to cry.

"Co jest nie tak?" she asked, dreading the answer. *What's wrong?*

"Nie wiem," her aunt responded. *I don't know.*

The Cat Woman regained her feet with Gosia's baby in her arms. "C'mon now," she coaxed the infant. "Time to wake up."

"Co jest nie tak?"

"Nie wiem."

"C'mon now... Wake up, little one."

Suddenly the baby began to wail, his cry rising above the radio broadcast. The Cat Woman smiled, then looked at Gosia, her smile melting into a frown.

"What are you doing down there? Get back into bed."

Ewa helped Gosia resettle in bed as the Cat Woman dried the infant—a boy—and then swaddled him in a soft blanket. Afterward she handed him to his mother, Gosia's eyes widening at his appearance.

"Co jest nie tak z jego głowa?" *What's wrong with his head?*

Ewa chuckled. "He's fine," she replied in Polish. "Poor fellow got squeezed out like toothpaste. His little conehead will be round as a cabbage by morning."

"Have you picked a name?" the Cat Woman asked.

Gosia understood the question without need for translation. "Józef," she replied. "Józef Farley Pietkowski."

The Cat Woman's eyes narrowed as if the baby's name had disinterred a disturbing memory. Then her expression relaxed and she extracted a vial of water from her pocket. She poured some into her hand and rubbed it on the baby's head.

"Welcome to America, Józef," she said.

Gosia understood those words as well. She'd imagined the moment, anticipating the thrill and relief when her child was officially an American, the United States his home. Instead, she recalled the words of the man from the Jewish Agency. "A home is not walls and a roof," David Ben-Gurion had philosophized after the pilot, Nowak, returned with him to Yorkshire, bringing along the promise of a homeland in Palestine. More interested in Antoni's services, Ben-Gurion had nevertheless focused his recruiting efforts on Gosia. "A home is the place your ancestors called home, as well," he'd asserted. "That your descendants can forever call home." The little man had contended that Gosia and Antoni's child would never be truly accepted in America. "Disowned, displaced, and disavowed, he or she will forever be a foreigner," he'd warned. "A refugee, a person without a country." After he left Gosia had vehemently argued against embracing his vision.

But now...

Little Józef began to squirm impatiently, his lips puckering as he searched for his mother's teat. Gosia freed up a breast and let the baby draw her nipple into his mouth. He immediately began to suckle, and although her milk had yet to come in, he seemed content to simply have his mother's familiar heartbeat in his ear. The girl on the radio had returned to the microphones, resuming her song as Gosia marveled at the miracle of her child—the tangled rasp of hair like Antoni's, the cupid's bow mouth like hers, the layers of cells upon cells upon more cells, all of them put perfectly into place over the course of nine months. It was a wonder that both mesmerized and baffled her and Gosia wished Antoni were there to share the moment.

She looked up at the Cat Woman. Madness was already stealing back into the wild-haired woman's eyes, her flirtation with reality near its end. Gosia was profoundly grateful to the crazy lady in the long winter coat and wanted her to embrace sanity long enough to hear about the dreams Józef's parents had for a child with actual possibilities—to understand why he would be an American who did not live in America. But she couldn't talk—her throat too full, the Cat Woman's time in the real world too short.

"Thank you," Gosia managed in English.

A different singer came on the radio, her voice more mature—a woman who had clearly known heartache. Gosia listened, trying to pick out words she understood. Her nipple slipped from Józef's mouth and he began to squirm impatiently. She helped him find it and settle, then resumed listening to the plaintive voice on the radio, at the same time watching her newborn son suckle, pulling harder and harder until she sensed the faintest rush of milk trickling from her breast.

Zimmer

"I give up, you idiot!" Zimmer barked at the American, speaking in German. He detached the strap from his rucksack and used it to fashion a tourniquet around his leg, grunting with pain as he tightened it. An exchange of words in German and English followed, neither man understanding the other until Zimmer cursed.

"Gott verdammt!"

He heard the American laugh, then again grow quiet, giving up the night to the odd static of crowd noise distantly emanating from the base loudspeakers. Zimmer's leg throbbed but he welcomed it. Most men who'd died fighting alongside him had been instantly killed or succumbed to their wounds within seconds. Those who'd taken longer felt no pain just before the end. His pain was reassuring. He was not dying.

He touched the entry wound on the front of his thigh, checking for active bleeding. Braun, the butcher's son, had shown Zimmer and Karl Janning the spots they should cut in hand-to-hand combat with field knives. "Go for the crease, inner mid-thigh. Cut the femoral artery and a man will bleed out in seconds," he'd taught them. Zimmer's wound was at the edge of his thigh, away from nerves and vessels. The blood had already begun to congeal. He carefully probed, breathing a sigh of relief when he found an exit wound. The bullet had gone all the way through without hitting anything vital.

The American called out again, one word understandable. Zimmer had studied both French and Spanish in school and was fluent in both. He shouted back.

"Mexikaner?"

More words were exchanged followed by a few moments of silent indecision on both sides. Then the American called out again. "Hey, Fritz… Manos arriba."

Lying on his back, Zimmer raised his hands and waited. Moments later a face peered down at him. The American was young…much younger than Zimmer. *A boy, really*, he thought, suddenly exasperated.

"I was giving up and you shot me, idiot," he griped in Spanish.

The American's reply was also in Spanish. "Are you armed?"

Am I armed? I gave up, you moron! What do you think?

Zimmer shook his head and the American told him to lower his arms. Then the young airman re-holstered his weapon and knelt, gently examining Zimmer's thigh, front and back. He tightened the tourniquet, afterward helping the wounded man to his feet, and together, they worked their way across the slope, down the knee-high embankment, and onto the road. With the American half-carrying him, they moved toward the airfield. Along the way, the girl on the radio resumed singing.

"'O'er the land…'"

The American sighed with relief, then told Zimmer—first in English and then in Spanish—that it was his sister. His voice was tinged with pride.

Zimmer nodded. "Good singer," he replied in Spanish.

"Ustedes?" the American asked as they approached a bend in the road. "Hermanos o hermanas?" *You…brothers or sisters?*

"No…sólo yo." *Just me.*

Moving slowly they breached the curve in the road. The gates to Feucht Airfield were now visible, high spotlights creating a row of halos along the entire length of the perimeter fence. The American's sister had finished her radio performance and Billie Holiday's voice now drifted through the air from the base loudspeakers. Zimmer looked at his watch face.

"Es pasada medianoche," he said. "La guerra…es terminó." *It's past midnight. The war is over.*

"Solo en Europa." *Only in Europe.*

"Luego, a Japan?" Zimmer asked. *Next, to Japan?*

"No…aqui por un tiempo, entonces a la casa." *Here for a while, then home.*

Zimmer nodded. "Gut," he said, reverting to German. He was breathing more heavily with the effort to walk on his wounded leg. They slowed.

"Que me pasa ahora?" he asked. *What happens to me now?*

"No eres SS, verdad?" the American teased. *You're not SS, are you?*

Braun had taught Zimmer other words in English. He used them.

"Fuck the SS. Fuck Hitler."

The American chuckled. "Entonces a casa para ti tambien," he said. *Then home for you too.*

"Gut."

"Yeah…gut."

Two guards emerged as they neared the posthouse adjacent to the gates, their rifles aimed at the approaching figures. One called out. The American answered and the sentries lowered their weapons, the heftier of the two coming to help. Supported by the Americans, Zimmer moved through the gates as Miss Holiday sang "God Bless the Child." He was a fan of the American singer. He'd heard the recording many times and softly hummed along as she delivered the lyrics in her distinctive vibrato. The Wehrmacht soldier knew he'd been lucky on this night. The bullet had missed bone and nerve. It hadn't hit a major blood vessel. He'd not bled to death. And he'd surrendered to an American rather than the Russians—to a man who seemed like a decent sort.

Zimmer began to imagine a reunion of the two soldiers long after the war was forgotten—a pair of old men sitting beside a lake in the open air, sharing pictures of children and grandchildren, smoking strong tobacco in pipes, and drinking dark beer in mugs. Ilse would bring them bread and sausages. The American's sister would sit nearby, strumming a guitar and singing a German folk song learned for the occasion. Evening would come and the two former enemies would ponder the emergence of the moon and stars, each quietly thanking God for putting a good man on the roadway and another good man in the forest on that long-ago, dimly moonlit night.

Zimmer tested his weight on the wounded leg. It hurt and he again let the two Americans half-tote him. The infirmary was just ahead. Beyond it—what was in store—was uncertain and Zimmer returned to his dream, praying it would someday be real; that all of it would eventually come true.

Riley

Riley dragged them through an obstacle course of feet, legs, and fallen bodies, the thick fabric of his overcoat protecting his elbows. Near the steps leading to the stage he and Jenny regained their feet and faced each other, fingers intertwined. Riley looked into her eyes.

"I love you," he said.

Jenny leaned forward and whispered in his ear. "You have to run now, Riley."

"Jenny!"

They both looked to the voice. From thirty feet away Jenny's father and the two cops pushed their way through the crowd. Jenny turned back to face Riley.

"Run," she repeated.

And Riley did. He ran, disappearing into a crowd that first swallowed him and then spat him out near a subway entrance. Sweating profusely he shed the Cat Woman's heavy overcoat, scrambled down steps to the lower concourse, and hopped the turnstile. A train was waiting, its doors gaping open. He boarded, the doors whooshed shut, and the subway carriage began to move.

The car was empty save one passenger who eerily resembled the Cat Woman, her hair in disarray, her fingernails chipped, her eyes feverish. Riley remained standing. Panting and soaked in perspiration he gripped a metal pole as the woman glared at him. At the next stop she made a great show of leaving, pinching her nose shut with two fingers as she passed him to exit, then offering the extended middle finger of one hand as the doors glided shut.

"You stink!" she yelled from the platform as the train pulled away.

Alone as the subway car moved down the tracks, Riley released his hold on the pole. He'd learned to keep his balance in rough water on the Lakes and instinctively shifted his weight back and forth or to and fro when the car swayed or leaned into a curve. Stops came and went. The train exited the tunnel for a few blocks in Harlem, then nosed back underground. There was a scheduled delay of nearly two minutes at the north end of the line. Then they were off again, heading for the bottom of Manhattan Island. At the Fifty-Ninth Street station, three passengers boarded: an older man too thick in the waist for his trousers and a pair of young women sporting identical hairstyles: side rolls lipping over their foreheads like a pair of sock puppets, the rest hanging loosely to the backs of their necks. They were laughing when they boarded, pausing to eye him before going back to their conversation.

"And then he said... Ha, ha, ha!"

"And then I told him... Ha, ha, ha!"

The man got off after two stops, the young women at the third. More stations followed—the doors opening and closing to no one—and Riley began to wonder if he'd died in Times Square and was now in the purgatory Pastor Wondercheck had predicted for him.

"There are no imbeciles in Heaven, boy."

At the South Ferry station the doors stayed open, but Riley

didn't move as a short but substantial conductor approached, his neck and fingers thick, his chest a barrel. He was in shirtsleeves, his uniform jacket slung over one arm.

"End of the line, buddy. You gotta get off," he said.

"I know. I ain't no imbecile."

The conductor peered more closely at him.

"You got someplace to go, son?" he asked. Riley didn't answer and the trainman took his arm and tugged gently. "I'm sorry, but you gotta get off, boy," he said. "Car's gotta be serviced." He escorted him onto the platform and then released his arm, following Riley's eyes to a huge recruiting mural on the wall. It displayed a sailor about Riley's age manning a bow-mounted machine gun on a coast guard cutter. The sailor was grinning.

"You headed for the recruiting station?" the conductor asked.

Riley hesitated, then nodded.

"It's not the navy, you know. It's the coast guard. You sure that's what you want?"

"I know what it is. I ain't stupid."

"Take it easy, son. I was just making sure."

"The army gimme a test. Sixty-nine was for dummies. I got a seventy. I passed. I just couldn't take my gun apart and put it back together. That's all. I worked the Lakes with Pap. I know boats. I could do what that guy in the picture is doin'. I ain't stupid."

The conductor chuckled. "I'm sorry, boy. Don't get worked up. I get it. You're not stupid." He shifted his gaze back to the mural. "Coast guard's a good choice. Better to be on a boat than in the mud. I did my time in the infantry. You know...the Great War...the first one."

He waited for a response, then shrugged.

"Good luck to you, son," he said.

The conductor headed for the stairs leading to the street above. Riley watched for a few moments and then turned back to the mural with the grinning sailor. He *did* know boats. He'd loved the huge Great Lakes freighter—the churn of its massive turbines, the hiss of the steam when they were powered down, the slap of waves against the hull at night, the melancholy horn across the water when they encountered another ship in the fog. The boat in the mural was smaller than a freighter. It was clean and white, the sailor happy.

What will Jenny think when I show up in a uniform?

A disembodied voice startled him, announcing another arrival as the car to be serviced began to move, the coast guard sailor in the mural reflected in its smudged window. Riley glanced up the tunnel. The advancing beam of a headlight searched the tracks. Moments later the bright eye of the approaching subway appeared and then eased into the station, gliding to a stop. The doors whooshed open and a raggedy man exited, glancing suspiciously at Riley before dashing to a trash can as if in a race. He reached it and rummaged through the garbage, disinterring the remains of a sandwich partially wrapped in brown butcher's paper. "Aha!" he shouted, holding it up. He looked around, face flushed with triumph. But he was alone, Riley Blaine already on the steps that led to the street and the open air above.

Antoni

Antoni pushed a switch on the wall and the light inside Stangl's cell came on. Wearing prison fatigues sans patches or emblems, the former commandant at Sobibor stood in the center of his cage as if at attention, his arrogance undampened even as he squinted against the harsh light of the bare overhead bulb. Antoni unlocked the door, then pulled it open. He stepped inside and Stangl's eyes widened at the sight of the gun, his defiance wilting as he retreated into one of the unyielding cinderblock walls.

Come here, filthy Jew!

He began to babble in German, his words spilling out like blood from an open vein. "How is your wife…your Gosia?"

Antoni stiffened, his finger tightening on the trigger of the Luger.

"Please tell her hello from me…"

The voice of the American broadcaster, Farley Sackstead, suddenly echoed down the cellblock corridor from the guardroom radio. He spoke for a while, then gave up the airwaves to the singer. "'O'er the land…'"

Antoni had dreamt of this moment—alone with the White Death in a room from which there was no escape. He'd imagined Stangl tied to a chair and thought about the club he would use to break each of the bastard's fingers and toes, afterward moving on to ankles, knees, ribs, and finally, Stangl's squarish Aryan skull. As always, the dream ended badly: Stangl dead, Antoni ashamed.

Did you shit yourself, dirty Jew?

"Yes, give her my very best and be sure to tell her how happy I am that you both escaped," Stangl blathered. "*So* happy…so *very* happy."

Have you ever had such a man as I?

"We were all victims in a way, were we not? I was forced to obey orders. I did not want to, but I had no choice, did I?"

Stangl kept talking, his words melding into a machine-like buzz that eerily recalled for Antoni the rumble of the train's wheels across the tracks on the way to Sobibor. Antoni had killed three men there, more while fighting with the Polish Home Army. They were enemies. It was war. He'd felt no remorse. He would feel none now.

"You understand, don't you, Antoni? We're done with him."

"Bitte," Stangl sobbed, falling to his knees, hands covering his face.

"Hör auf zu reden!" Antoni barked. *Stop talking!*

The girl on the radio finished and a different voice began to waft down the corridor from the guardroom: the American chanteuse, Billie Holiday. Antoni tipped his head to listen. Her song, "God Bless the Child," seemed a promise and recalled for him a different vow, one made by David Ben-Gurion. The little politician had come to Yorkshire with Nowak, the Polish airman, the tiny giant's devotion dwarfing the celebrity of the ace pilot despite his diminutive stature. Barely five feet tall with wild gray-white hair that not so much grew from his head as was sprayed from it, Ben-Gurion had pledged to create a Jewish state in Palestine. He'd wanted Antoni and Gosia to join him.

"You can be part of a new beginning... Have something of your own in a land of your own."

Antoni touched the scar on his forehead, put there in Stangl's bivouac because pride had transiently overwhelmed his will to live. He'd made a promise that day. Tomorrow would come, he'd told Stangl. And now, tomorrow for the White Death had arrived.

"Bitte..."

Antoni pulled back the hammer on the pistol. Then he again hesitated, inexplicably visited by an intuition that he was a father; that four thousand miles away Gosia had delivered their child. The gun in his hand dipped slightly, his finger easing from the trigger.

"Bitte...bitte."

"Best to put him behind you."

Antoni lowered his gun arm until it dangled at his side as Stangl continued to blubber, his words incoherent.

"You can be part of a new beginning..."

Antoni took a deep breath and released it. Then he pointed the Luger at the bunk shoved against one wall and fired three shots into the pillow. Feathers erupted and he backed out of the cell. He closed and locked the door, shuttered the view slit, and turned off the light.

In the guardroom he found the drawling sergeant leaning back in a chair, his feet atop the room's small desk. Antoni placed the key to Stangl's cell next to the guard's large boots.

"Where is the major?" he asked.

The sergeant nodded at a door leading to the parade ground outside the stockade. "Couldn't do it, right?" he said. He went on when Antoni didn't respond. "I figgered as much. You Hebes ain't got it in ya to fight."

"Goodbye, sergeant," Antoni said, crossing to the door.

Outside, the night was warm and breathless, the grounds

open, a light breeze reassuring. The major was waiting, a cigarette dangling from his lips as he studied a sky filled with stars. Antoni handed him the Luger. The major removed the silencer, then holstered the weapon and they headed for the airfield and a plane that would return them to Nuremberg. Billie Holiday's "God Bless the Child" followed them—her lyrics both augury and epitaph—wafting through an open window in the stockade, her melancholy warble delivering an anthem truer for the escapee from Sobibor than America's "The Star-Spangled Banner." Walking silently along a path lined with white stones that cut between the various buildings on the base, they reached the airfield. Just past an access gate, the silhouette of their plane loomed in the darkness.

"I didn't do it," Antoni told the major.

"I don't understand," the officer replied. He held the gate open for Antoni to pass through.

"I know, major," Antoni said as they continued on toward their aircraft with Miss Holiday's voice fading into the night and the stockade that caged Franz Stangl farther and farther behind them.

Afterword

While the depiction of Franz Stangl in this book is a figment of my imagination, the man known as the White Death was very real. Commandant of the Sobibor death camp from 28 April 1942 to the end of August that same year, he was detained by the U.S. Army in 1945 and briefly imprisoned in Linz, Austria, the site of his fictional scenes in this book. In 1948 he escaped and fled to Italy. With the assistance of disgraced Catholic bishop Alois Hudal, he then slipped into Syria and made his way to Brazil. In 1961 a West German court issued an arrest warrant, but Stangl avoided extradition for six more years. Eventually his appeals were exhausted and he was returned to Germany to stand trial. Accused of the murders of nearly one million people, he was found guilty and sentenced to imprisonment for the remainder of his natural life. He died in 1971 while still incarcerated.

My fictional airman, Jimmy Doyle, is based on the life of my late friend, Max Ault, who manned a belly turret machine gun on a B-17 Flying Fortress when just seventeen years old. After V-E Day, Max stayed in Europe where his plane and its crew participated in Project Casey Jones, an aerial-mapping operation that targeted Europe, Iceland, and North Africa. Project Casey Jones remained classified for many years, even though it was downgraded from "Top Secret" to "Confidential" in 1946. Indeed, as he approached the end of his life, Max still knew very little about the photos he'd taken from his cramped Plexiglas capsule until my wife, Pam, managed to obtain a freshly declassified report from an Air Force historian. Putting together a monograph for our friend that included pictures of Max's plane and the young airman in his uniform, she finished it in time for Max to read about his exploits before his death in 2015.

The character of Farley Sackstead is based on the lives of two men: Edward R. Murrow, the famed radio and television journalist, whose *This is London* broadcasts kept America informed during World War II; and William L. Shirer, one of the famed "Murrow boys" along with such notables as Eric Sevareid and Howard K. Smith. After many years as a foreign correspondent Shirer published *The Rise and Fall of the Third Reich* in 1960. It remains the definitive account of the ascension of Adolf Hitler and National Socialism in Germany and a warning to all of how easily fear, bigotry, vengefulness, and apathy can allow fascism to smother genuine freedom.

ACKNOWLEDGMENTS

My thanks to writers Leslie Gunnerson, Chris Dempsey, and Mike Christian for their valuable input as I wrote this book. Thanks also to advance readers Karla Huebner, Jeff Schnader, and Elizabeth Winthrop. My gratitude to Regal House Publishing and Jaynie Royal for rolling the dice on me a fourth time. As always, thanks and love to my wife, Pam, and to my children and grandchildren who continue to amaze me.